HOUSES FALLEN

Houses of the Dead: Book Two

LEAH R CUTTER

Houses Fallen
Houses of the Dead: Book Two
Copyright © 2020 Leah Cutter
All rights reserved
Published by Knotted Road Press
www.KnottedRoadPress.com

ISBN: 978-1-64470-189-8

Cover Art:

ID 26691751 © Dusan Kostic | Dreamstime.com

Cover and interior design copyright © 2020 Knotted Road Press
http://www.KnottedRoadPress.com

Reviews

It's true. Reviews help me sell more books. If you've enjoyed this story, please consider leaving a review of it on your favorite site.

Come someplace new...

Are you a traveler? Do you enjoy exploring strange new worlds, new cultures, new people?

Journey into the various lands envisioned by Leah Cutter.

Sign up for my newsletter and I'll start you on your travels with a free copy of my book, *The Island Sampler.*

http://www.LeahCutter.com/newsletter/

Also by Leah R Cutter

Forgotten Gods

A Wind Blown Torment

A Stone Strewn Clash

A Sea Washed Victory

Tanish Empire Trilogy

The Glass Magician

The Desert Heart

The Ghost Dog

The Cassie Stories

Poisoned Pearls

Tainted Waters

Spoiled Harvest

Bloodied Ice

The Witch's Progress

Circle of Air

Circle of Water

Circle of Fire

Circle of Earth

Seattle Trolls

The Changeling Troll

The Princess Troll

The Fairy-Bridge Troll

The Troll-Demon War

The Troll-Human War

The Troll-Troll War

The Shadow Wars Trilogy

The Raven and the Dancing Tiger

The Guardian Hound

War Among the Crocodiles

The Clockwork Fairy Kingdom

The Clockwork Fairy Kingdom

The Maker, the Teacher, and the Monster

The Dwarven Wars

The Chronicles of Franklin

Franklin Versus The Popcorn Thief

Franklin Versus The Soul Thief

Franklin Versus The Child Thief

Huli Intergalactic - Science/Space Fantasy

Origins

The Strawberry Girl

Contemporary Fantasy

Siren's Call

The Immortals' War

Mountains
House of Crystal
Nyati
House of Pearl
House of Gold
Ocean
Yawatan
House of Cobalt
Jinyi

Chapter One

HOUSE OF CRYSTAL

MENHAPTU PAUSED before entering the stairs leading down to the Chamber of Crystals. He held an actual burning, lighted torch in one hand, the sound of the lit wood hissing and distracting. The heat, also, was unusual. Magical lights were neither hot nor cold.

But the world was no longer what it once had been, even what it had been the week before.

He glanced down at his robes. They were too short and fell just below his knee. The cool air from the chamber below sent goosebumps across the exposed calves. The sleeves were too short, the finely embroidered cuff ending mid-forearm. In addition, the robes were too voluminous, and had to be belted. He felt like a child playing dress up, having borrowed someone else's clothes.

Then again, these robes had been worn by his predecessor, Haptomi (long may he rest in the Golden Lands).

There hadn't been time to make Menhaptu his own set after he'd been shoved into the head of the Temple of Truth.

And someone needed to go down to the Chamber of Crystals and ask what was going on.

At least the robes he wore were made out of beautiful off-white fabric with wide stripes of gold woven into it. It suited his pale skin and freckles, as well as his short, auburn colored hair and his steel gray eyes.

However, it still wasn't fair. He shouldn't have to be the one to do this.

But there was no denying that Ibitsima, as well as her entire retinue, had been slaughtered while visiting the House of Cobalt for the annual festival, just three days before.

Just as there was no denying that the land had yet to settle on a new LandHolder.

Someone had to go ask the Chamber of Crystals *something*. It would be presumptuous to ask who the next LandHolder should be. Even the Land didn't know that.

But why had this outcome not been foreseen? That was the question on everyone's mind.

The elders at the Temple of Truth considered it an inappropriate question.

Menhaptu was going to ask it anyway.

He breathed in the smell of the underground cavern, flowing up the stairs. It felt cold, like a foreboding tomb.

Menhaptu stiffened his spine and began his descent down the steep stone stairs. His heart pounded loudly. Despite the cold, sweat started to form under his arms and at the base of his spine. His knees felt weak as he carefully descended, the steps jarring and unforgiving.

Darkness ate at the light he carried. The halo cast by the torch diminished until Menhaptu could barely see the steps.

The chamber below was filled with inky night, waters that might overwhelm him and steal his soul.

However, he couldn't rely on his landsense to direct him. All magic was unpredictable, and would remain so in the lands of the House of Crystal until a new LandHolder was chosen.

If you, say, tried to light a candle, you might instead douse it with water. Or maybe slice the candle in half as if you'd just thrown a knife. Or perhaps even melt it complete to a stub.

Since the magic had been running out of the land already, people were vaguely prepared. Long wooden matchsticks were used to strike a flame and light candles. As it was summer, people complained of being too hot, no longer able to call up cool breezes. Goods perished quickly without the ability to keep them chilled.

Menhaptu didn't want to consider what the winter would be like with no heated stones.

The stairs ended abruptly. Menhaptu took a stumbling step.

Really, he shouldn't be the one to do this. He'd only been in the chamber once before, when he'd first been initiated into the Temple of Truth. One of the older, more experienced priests should have taken this duty, been nominated as the head of the Temple of Truth.

They'd thrust it on him instead, as Haptomi had been his personal mentor. That didn't mean much—Menhaptu had seen the elder priest maybe once a month, and then only for a short time, answering a set list of questions, not really talking with the man.

The other priests hadn't chosen him for the position because of some hidden talent. No, they'd done it because he was the youngest, barely twenty-five, as well as the one with the least powerful family.

No one knew what would happen when the Land finally chose a new LandHolder. Since it wasn't going to be one of Ibitsima's family—as she, her sister, and all their children had been killed—it could be anyone.

Even an existing LandHolder, from another land.

Which meant that the Temple of Truth in the House of Crystal might be subsumed by the other LandHolder's temple. The head of Crystal's Temple of Truth would lose all power. Most, if not all, of the higher-level priests and priestesses would be encouraged to retire.

Menhaptu might be the head priest for only a short time, while the others would hide among the ranks and still be associated with the temple.

Not if they survived this crisis and Menhaptu was still in charge.

But that was for another day.

For now, Menhaptu had to make it through the inky darkness that clung to him like a cold mist, then into the Chamber of Crystals to ask his question.

And survive it.

If the chamber would even talk with him.

Menhaptu wanted to press out with his landsense, to see if the chamber really did lie ahead of him. He was afraid of what would happen, though. Would the land reach up and overwhelm his senses, leaving him passed out on the floor until he woke up hours from now? That had happened to more than one poor individual who hadn't been able to refrain after the death of a previous LandHolder.

Or would the land turn its back on him, and he'd start the downward trend into the Abandonment, the wasting disease that frequently took the elderly when they could no longer feel the land? That had already started with some of the young people in the capital city of Nyati.

Menhaptu stubbornly shuffled his feet forward, using the torch to light his path.

Wait, was that something glowing up ahead?

The coldness of the underground chamber pulled back.

The light thrown by the torch increased, until Menhaptu could finally start seeing a few feet ahead of him.

There. He'd been walking directly toward the opening of the Chamber of Crystals. Though he hadn't been consciously using his landsense, maybe it had been trying to subtly guide him anyway.

It hadn't been the ghosts. They'd practically vanished from the House of Crystal. Those who were most sensitive would catch the occasional glimpse of one. But most of the ghosts had disappeared.

Another flickering light shone in front of him, followed by more.

Menhaptu's knees felt weak with relief.

The chamber appeared to be awake. Hopefully, that would be a good thing.

He stepped through the round opening into the actual Chamber of Crystals itself, stopping almost immediately.

Crystal spires of rock jutted out from the floor, the walls, the rounded ceiling. Some were the size of Menhaptu's outstretched hand, others were three feet or more tall. The chamber was round, just like the inside of a geode. Menhaptu knew better than to reach out or touch any of the crystals. They were sharp enough to slice his skin.

A parade of bright colors marched around the room, ribbons of blue, red, green, orange, and yellow. It soothed his soul to see magic working this way.

Maybe they could survive this time of uncertainty if the Chamber of Crystals was still operational.

Menhaptu belatedly remembered to start his hymns, singing praises to the God Djediese in his rainbow cloak, who brought magic to the world of men. He also thanked the Goddess Orlorg for making the earth fruitful, the God Xiuma for their continued good fortune, as well as the Goddess Morta, entreating her to let them survive this storm.

When he finished, he heard a faint hum fill the chamber. The changing colors slowed, growing together, until it appeared that sheets moving from one section to the next.

If Haptomi's notes were accurate, it was a sign that the chamber was ready for a question.

As magic had seeped out of the world, the chamber had frequently responded in a hum, but had refused to answer any questions, those last few months when Haptomi had come down to the chamber.

Menhaptu hoped that his luck might be different than his predecessor's.

He drew a deep breath, then sang out his question in a loud voice.

Who is responsible for our lack of foretelling?

Colors suddenly blared. A high pitched humming filled the area. Menhaptu took a step back, prepared to turn and run should the Chamber of Crystals suddenly start shooting crystal spires at him, trying to kill him.

The humming abruptly dropped to a quieter tone. Colors drained out of the walls, until all the crystals shone with a milky white. In front of Menhaptu's feet, the crystals jutting up and blocking access from the interior of the chamber, just melted away. A tinny smell filled the area, and the air grew warmer.

Was it a trap? Had the Chamber of Crystals decided that Menhaptu's question was so outrageous that it needed to kill him?

He didn't know. He had to trust that the gods had a plan for him, though.

Hesitatingly, Menhaptu took a step forward. Then another. Then another.

The humming in the chamber took on an expectant note.

What was he supposed to be doing? He looked around, marveling at the beauty of the crystals surrounding him. They were glorious, yet completely alien. He was in a foreign world, now, cut off from everything manmade.

One more step. Menhaptu stopped.

What was that? There, to the right? Hidden from the entrance by a massive series of crystal spires?

At first, he thought it was a bare spot among the crowded crystals, where the brown earth was tolerated, a round patch about three feet across.

Only when he looked more closely could he see that it was actually filled with smaller crystals that had all turned brown.

Fine black lines marred the beauty of the rocks. They looked brittle and corrupted.

The whiteness that filled the crystals surrounding the brown spot shrank back. It pushed forward again, but was blocked by the dark spot. The area was now slightly larger than it had been.

Menhaptu gasped.

The brown spot, that place of decay, was growing. The Chamber of Crystals was fighting it, trying to retain its colors and its glory.

But it was slowly being taken over by something else. Something from deep in the heart of the earth.

Something demonic.

Menhaptu shivered and raced from the chamber as if all of the Goddess Morta's demons were chasing him. He sprinted across the blackness. Wet threads broke against his face and hands, as if he'd been walking through a fog. The smell of decay and rotting bones filled the air.

Menhaptu didn't stop until he reached the top of the stairs. And only then to slam shut the door that protected the stairs.

He drew a shuddering breath, leaning his back against the shut door.

At least now they knew why none had predicted the fate of the LandHolder.

The Chamber of Crystals itself was corrupt.

And the rest of the land would fall under the sway of the demons soon, if the people of the land didn't stop it.

Chapter Two
HOUSE OF COBALT

WANHO, the demon who shared the LandHolder Kinaki's body, smiled as they looked out on the court. Any of the Holders who hadn't supported him had already been removed—either eaten or possessed.

There were still a few "pure" souls, as it were, standing before him, those who didn't need a demon's touch to do his bidding.

The room had changed during the two years that Wanho had been present. Beautiful pots of fragrant flowers filled the corners. Vines draped across the walls, giving the formerly sterile room the feeling of a jungle, something few from the House of Cobalt knew of. The windows were covered with a thick film, meant to hold in the warm air and prevent any of the living from escaping. Wooden floors had been replaced with fresh, good dirt and limestone. A huge hearth, piled high with heated rocks, had remained unchanged except from the color, growing from a stark white to a dim gray.

Kinaki wore one of the looser robes today, as Wanho had felt himself growing with all the deaths. Kinaki stood taller than he once did. Soon, he would be a giant among men. The robe was a pleasing light blue color, with black and red streaks, like ashes and blood. Flowers festooned the cloth. The living were really so clever at that.

Wanho knew the myths, how demons like himself had at one point been warriors, placed underground by the Goddess Morta herself to test new souls when they descended. If the soul proved itself worthy, it was supposed to be allowed to pass to the River Guanaliki, then follow its course to the grand ocean of light and be carried away to the Golden Lands.

Maybe at some time in the past, Wanho had performed such duties. But as the centuries had gone by, he'd grown bitter that he could never reach the River Guanaliki himself. His position was forever fixed under the earth.

He could never rest. Could never find the ocean of light or be allowed to pass into the Golden Lands.

Since there was no hope, he was determined to take over all the underworld. To force the Goddess Morta to see his great command, to draw him into her bosom as one of her chosen.

The demons who were slain stayed dead. They didn't return to the underworld. Their souls were lost, though Wanho knew it wasn't that great of a loss. The light that had sustained them was pitiful and small.

Unlike the living who stood before him. They shone like a full moon, silvery and strong. Even those who also bore a demonic soul.

Kinaki was saying something, talking about how they now had this great opportunity to expand the lands for the House of Cobalt. It amused Wanho to let the LandHolder believe that he was in charge.

When really, it was Wanho who pulled all the strings.

Still, Kinaki had good ideas. He knew the living much better than Wanho did.

Had Wanho ever been alive? When he'd been under the earth he'd dreamed of the sunlight and flowers. However, what he saw never matched his imagination. No, he'd possibly never been alive, but only born out of the will of the Goddess Morta.

Who'd then given him a thankless task and turned her back on him.

All the gods had turned their backs on their creation.

It was time for the living as well as the dead to demand an accounting.

Court was shortly dismissed. Kinaki stood and stretched. Such an odd thing for the living to do! Wanho could make all of their shared body's muscles dance. To grow or shrink down. He didn't see the point in all that exercise that Kinaki *still* insisted on doing every morning, even as they prepared for war.

Only after Kinaki sat back down were the CollierHolders issued into the room.

Surrounded, of course, by Wanho's own WarHolders.

At first, Kinaki had appeared to love the idea of dedicated WarHolders, of making permanent war with the other LandHolders. The other LandHolders had been appalled, however. It wasn't how they conducted their battles. Kinaki hadn't had questions, afterward, but he had felt a touch uneasy, at least as far as Wanho could tell.

All fighting was to increase a LandHolder's share of the land: it wasn't to make war itself. It was why each house had its own name for the top commanders, such as PearlHolder or VeinHolder.

As all of the southern border of the House of Cobalt faced the barbarians, those who had no landsense at all, Kinaki had more warriors than the other houses, as well as additional ranks, such as the PitHolders, ShaftHolders, and even CinderHolders.

Today, though, it was just the top commanders, those who would carry the great battles into the lands of the other houses, starting with the House of Gold. They shared a long, unmanned border to the north.

Yes, Unnir had raised a defensive shield against the first attacks sent by the House of Cobalt—that damned golden curtain that lay all along the border between their two lands. She wouldn't be able to hold out for too long, though. Not given how those in her own household plotted against her.

Once Kinaki had consumed the lands from the House of Gold, he would push on. Probably take the House of Crystal next, as its LandHolder would still be new and untested.

Then, he would turn his attention to the House of Pearl. Hills separated the lands, which meant that the House of Pearl was cut off from the others.

With no one to come to their aid, they too would fall. Alone.

And Wanho, through Kinaki, would rule all of the lands, both aboveground as well as below.

Let the gods see that he was serious. Let them come down and try to wrest it from him.

He had plans for them, too.

Wanho listened for a while to Kinaki's rousing speech about how they would ultimately be the one LandHolder, as was their divine right, having risen from the dead.

It wasn't Kinaki, though, who would control all the lands. It would be Wanho.

Though he couldn't exist outside of Kinaki's body. None of the demons could.

That didn't mean he wasn't thinking about it. Experimenting with towering plants, seeing how much consciousness he could bring to one of them.

The only note that struck him as off was when Kinaki split the troops. What was he doing?

Are you certain? Wanho whispered into Kinaki's ear. Though Wanho could cut off the air to Kinaki's throat to stop him from speaking, he'd learned not too. Kinaki couldn't be seen as weak, at least not by those in the court.

Instead, he'd pose a question that Kinaki would generally answer as he was speaking to the others.

"By keeping the gains we've made to the south, all the land we've acquired there, we will be stronger in our attack to the north," Kinaki said.

Ah. That made sense. The LandHolder would be able to draw more magical power if he had more land at his disposal. And Wanho had learned that as soon as any of the troops were withdrawn from the barbarian lands, those people would attack and retake their fields.

Wanho nodded, more to himself than to anyone else. It was the other reason why he still needed Kinaki. The living were sneaky. In some ways, he felt they were much more devious than demons were. Yes, there were myths about clever puzzles, but none of the demons who Wanho knew would have been able to compose such tests.

Demons were straightforward. Their sole objective was to gain power for themselves.

Wanho had actually joked once about becoming the more corrupt of the two, as he had more needs now. He felt as if he could live on the colors of the earth, breathe them in like a fine stew. (Only Kinaki needed to eat, and his diet had slowly changed to something Wanho found more appropriate.) The scent of the many flowers carried him away. The feel of solid ground beneath his feet delighted him, and he always sought more.

For now, both Wanho and Kinaki had the same primary goal: to acquire as much power as possible.

Once they controlled all the lands, their goals, as well as their paths, might diverge.

And maybe by that point, Wanho would no longer need Kinaki's body.

A poor demon could only hope.

Chapter Three
HOUSE OF GOLD

UNNIR SLEPT BADLY, of course. There were never any peaceful dreams for her, not with the constant testing of the southern border that ran between her lands and the House of Cobalt.

Soon, either later that day or the next, Kinaki would send his warriors and his demons to battle her VeinHolders and their fighters.

She would defend her lands with her last dying breath.

Which might occur much sooner than she'd originally planned.

She turned over in her lonely bed. She'd sent her husband to his own sleeping chambers early, not wanting to disturb him with her restlessness. She almost called him back now in the pre-dawn light, but decided instead to use the early morning to make more plans.

Her chambers were decidedly feminine. She'd made sure of that, since she'd inherited them from Uncle Yudur, the previous LandHolder. Soft pastel fabrics covered the walls. She'd redone the cold, white marble hearth in a warmer soapstone, gray with flecks of white and gold. Thick rugs with beautiful patterns of leaves and trees covered the stone floor. The sharp corners and angle that Yudur had delighted in were all smoothed over.

The window to the left of her bed showed another day dawning brightly outside. It felt so incongruous, that she should be facing a dark storm when the weather was so lovely. She felt the trees flush with leaves, the crops in the fields ripening, the trickling streams and peaceful rivers of her land all around her.

But to the south…

The golden curtain that she'd erected had discouraged the howling demons patrolling the House of Cobalt's side from crossing.

Everyone knew, though, that it was just a matter of time before they figured out a way to overcome the border. Emil and Vide had the most ideas when it came to that: how the demons, who didn't care if they lived or died, would pile on, one on top of the other, until finally there were too many for her to handle.

Either that, or it would be a multi-pronged attack, too many points at once for her to keep track of.

If there was anything good to come out of this war, it was that Emil and Vide had finally come to the realization that there was something bigger than their petty fighting. They needed to help her, for them all to work together, if the House of Gold was to survive.

Unnir sat up on her bed, pulling her knees up and resting her head against them. All was darkness before her. Torja, the head priestess of the Temple of Truth, had finally admitted that the entire temple had been lying to the LandHolder, that none in the temple had been able to cast accurate auguries for a year or more.

So Unnir would have no hint as to where the demons

would attack first, where her VeinHolders should set their warriors.

Torja had finally healed since her last desperate vision. She'd burned her face horribly in order to obtain a vision and bring her LandHolder the news that Kinaki had been possessed by demons and that Darikuto, the LandHolder for the House of Pearl, had been the one who'd arranged for it.

The only LandHolder who Unnir might have been able to trust had been killed by Darikuto. Any winds that blew from the north across Unnir's land left her unsettled. The land there hadn't chosen a new LandHolder.

If she wasn't facing a devastating army from the south, Unnir might have journeyed north herself, seen if she could coax the uneasy land into settling across her shoulders.

It would have made her a force to be reckoned with. The other LandHolders had perceived her as weak, as she was the youngest of all of them. Emil and Vide's constant plotting and conniving hadn't helped.

In the next few days, she'd find out just how strong she actually was.

Hopefully, she'd be strong enough to survive.

Chapter Four
HOUSE OF PEARL

CHUYOKO LOOKED around the room where the other PearlHolders were seated on cushions on the floor, trying to figure out how to deal with those opposed to her.

Though officially all PearlHolders had the same rank, unofficially, they were actually split among three: SeedPearlHolders, LuminousPearlHolders, and BlackPearlHolders, indicating their ranks from lowest to highest.

Only the two dozen BlackPearlHolders were gathered that afternoon in the capital city of Yawatan, in Darikuto's strong hold. They were in a rough circle on a smooth wooden floor, each comfortably kneeling on a hard pillow. The walls were painted a light gray, like sea mist, with a few ink drawings of fish and waves hanging mid-wall. White paper shades covered the windows, providing the only light for the room.

The warriors in the room were brightly colored in comparison, wearing stiff, formal robes in blues, silvers, and blacks. No one wore a weapon, or any armor. There would be time enough for them to live in their armor, once this meeting was over and they marched off to war.

The men and women around her were well seasoned, hardened over the years through training and battles. Though the House of Pearl's lands didn't have much of a border with the barbarians to the south, as part of The Plan, Chuyoko had constantly been cycling warriors through battles down there over the years.

Training would only take a warrior so far. Sooner or later, they had to face an actual enemy.

Now, they would all be facing foes in the next few days.

Though many of the PearlHolders answered to Chuyoko, this group answered to itself. If possible, they tried to make all decisions through consensus. In order to rise to this rank, a warrior had to be able to listen to sound advice as well as give it.

Currently, Chuyoko wanted to shake a few of the supposedly wiser heads in the group, make them hear reason.

"No, we *must* leave a substantial force at the border with the House of Cobalt," she said again.

The warriors around her rustled as they shifted from side to side. No one wanted to be denied the easy glory (and plunder) they could achieve when they attacked the House of Crystal's lands.

Did the fools not realize that there was a much greater threat immediately east?

Chuyoko had seen her mistake early on in the conversation. She'd focused on sending warriors down to battle. Not BlackPearlHolders. Once they'd done their time, as it were, they'd stopped fighting.

She didn't expect anyone to train as she did.

They still needed to train harder.

She couldn't go back and correct the mistakes of the past. Couldn't even alter the plan that Darikuto had in place.

Instead, she needed to move forward and do the best with what she had.

"I understand your concern," said Ornishito. He was a didactic man, full of his own importance. Chuyoko would bet that he cheated when it came to the training that she expected every BlackPearlHolder to maintain, using his magic to aid his running and his combat instead of his physical strength.

He was one that she'd gladly put in the front lines when it came to attacking the House of Cobalt, which they would need to do. Soon.

"However, the House of Cobalt is focused on its northern border, not its western one," he said. "They aren't even maintaining a guard here."

"They don't need to," Chuyoko said. "The vegetation itself will do that for them. The vines have eyes. The sharp sticks that thrust out of the ground work as a barrier to keep them safe."

"We don't train to battle plants," Ornishito said. "We battle men."

"What about demons?" Chuyoko asked sweetly. "How many of those have you been fighting recently?"

Ornishito pressed his lips together and glared balefully at her. He hadn't been among those she'd taken to the annual festival. No, she'd left him with the *very* important job of guarding the capital city.

As if anyone would dare to approach Yawatan. Not yet, at any rate.

"The demons won't rest in their attacks on the House of Gold's lands," Chuyoko admitted. "Kinaki is focused on his northern border. However, he doesn't control those forces, no matter what the LandHolder may think. They're reckless. Undisciplined. And deadly."

"You believe that a group of demon warriors may break

off from the north and come this way, unbidden by their CollierHolders or WarHolders?" Naradiki asked. She was one of the older BlackPearlHolders, her hair silver, shorn short, styled with spikes across the top of her skull. Her skin looked like aged leather, stretched tightly across whipcord muscles. Black eyes still twinkled in a wrinkled face.

Chuyoko was stronger than Naradiki, due to her diligent training, but she doubted that any of the others were.

"The eastern border would be an easy target if we don't leave an extra force there. How far inland could a hostile group get if they overwhelmed our usual guards?" Chuyoko said.

"Pretty far," Naradiki said. "Very well. I volunteer for this position. My warriors and various Holders will perform our duty to the LandHolder in this way."

"Thank you," Chuyoko said, bowing her head low to the older woman who at least understood the threat.

Then again, Naradiki had also met them at the border after they'd fled from the lands of the House of Cobalt. She'd seen the injuries that Chuyoko's warriors bore.

Had heard the screams of the warriors waking them before dawn, nightmares and festering wounds taking them.

"Will anyone else volunteer for this honor?" Chuyoko asked, looking around the room again.

Three other BlackPearlHolders volunteered, roughly one-sixth of their entire force.

If she could have pushed the issue, she would have left over half at the border with the House of Cobalt.

There were no defenses awaiting them in the lands of the House of Crystal. The guard there were disorganized, unable to focus due to the death of their LandHolder, and the land itself not choosing a new Holder.

It would be easy to fight their way to the heart of that land, then defend Darikuto while he cast the spells necessary to either encourage the land to settle on him, or to wrestle control of the land from whoever it had chosen.

She understood that everyone wanted to be there when the House of Pearl took over the lands of the House of Crystal. It would be a momentous event. No one alive had seen such a thing. There had been four LandHolders for at least two centuries. Only in distant times had there been fewer than there were now.

Still, she didn't need such a strong force, not for the battles north.

No, it was better to leave most of her force behind, preparing for the real battle.

When they had to take over the lands of the House of Cobalt.

Chapter Five

HOUSE OF CRYSTAL

AKALINA WOKE in her bedroom in the palace. A silent chorus of ghosts lined the walls of her room.

"What do you want from me?" she demanded as she sat up, throwing back the covers which had been heaped high. Though it was summer, the palace was still cool, and the constant conglomeration of ghosts in her room brought its own chill.

She still wore her virginal white nightgown. She wasn't likely to wear any other kind. Now that she knew for certain that she was barren, no man would want to marry her, with or without her parent's conniving. At least her nightgown was warm, made out of soft cotton flannel, with the edges of the long sleeves and the collar embroidered with white flowers.

The ghosts didn't reply, even after she stalked up and down in front of them, glaring.

They never did.

They seemed to be expecting her to do…something. If only they would tell her!

She didn't know for certain, but she suspected this

particular group of ghosts to be the ones who'd conspired to make her attend them at the court of the ghosts three years before. Rosahaptu had given up her ghostly presence to take all of Akalina's future children.

They must have known, or had some inkling, that Ibitsima would be killed and the land, bereft.

However, the land would never settle on someone who couldn't bear heirs. That single source of power and consciousness had only wrapped itself around her for a brief time before flying off to find another, more suitable LandHolder.

Then, Yimifut had refused. Akalina still didn't know why. Had it been the cold? Or was it something else, something he'd foreseen?

Without a LandHolder, all of the land was unsettled. Magic was unpredictable, if it could be done at all.

Akalina was luckier than most. It wasn't her landsense but her awareness of the ghosts that allowed her to still perform magic, such as lighting a candle with the snap of her fingers or warming the rocks piled high in the hearth.

"What do you want me to do?" Akalina asked the silent ghosts one last time.

The ghosts didn't respond. Some looked directly at her, glaring. Others looked away, as if ashamed to meet her eyes.

Most of the ghosts who remained in her rooms were older. She could tell based on their colors. Instead of being like white, fluffy clouds, they were tinted brown, including the eldest who looked like tea-stained paper. Their faces, necks, and shoulders were all well-defined. Their bodies and legs were not. They floated on clouds, as it were.

It took will to remain a ghost, in the lands of the living, instead of traveling to the underworld and eventually to the Golden Lands.

Akalina still cared for them as best she could, despite

their continued silence. She lit the incense on her side table with a thought, the smoke billowing up and out for the ghosts to "sip."

Then she turned to her wardrobe, ready to dress for the day. No nurse attended her, not anymore. Akalina chose a light shirt, pale green like the first spring leaves, a loose black skirt that swept the floor, warm gray wool stockings, and boots. Likely she'd change into sandals later, but for now, she was still cold.

She knew that part of her chilled state was due to the ghosts. The other part, however, was from when the land had wrapped around her, colder than a wet blanket found out in the snow.

A shiver overtook her as she remembered. Was the land always that cold? How had Ibitsima been able to stand it? Or would the land have thawed and warmed once it had accepted her as LandHolder?

Akalina didn't like to think what would have happened if that cold had remained. Would it have colored her every thought? She'd never been accused of being a particularly warm or welcoming child, unlike her eldest sister Befery, whom everyone loved.

Would Akalina have grown cold and harsh? Everyone knew that becoming a LandHolder changed the person in fundamental ways. Everyone said that Ibitsima had grown more formidable, more like the huge mountains to the north. In the past, LandHolders had also been compared to gushing mountain streams—always excited and rushing around—as well as deep meadow lakes, calm and still.

When Akalina finished dressing, she looked back at the ghosts.

Normally, the ghosts formed a line to come and sip at the smoke from the incense she burned for them. She'd never been able to figure out the pecking order, if they took turns being first, or if there was some ranking she didn't understand.

Today, however, no long line of ghosts waited their turn in front of her altar.

Instead, a single ghost stood there. He was the oldest of them, at least a century old. Wosriufi. He'd been a CrystalHolder, a fierce warrior who, according to legends, had single-handedly held back the VeinHolders from the House of Gold who'd come to attack a small farmstead.

Now dead, he looked like a courtier, with a balding head, pudgy round face, button nose and flabby lips. Maybe he'd been a great warrior when he'd been young, but he'd aged, and not well, before he'd died.

A thick looking jacket rested on his shoulders. Akalina wondered if at one point it had been made from fine black wool. He wore a large medallion around his neck, a reward perhaps for his younger great deeds. The rest of his body was indistinct, made out of tea-stained clouds.

Akalina walked up to Wosriufi, waiting patiently as he finished. There wasn't much else for her to do but wait. Her fate would have been decided by Ibitsima and Haptomi when they'd returned.

As they were never to return, and a new LandHolder hadn't been selected, no one quite knew what to do with her.

She'd finally been able to arrange a meeting with Menhaptu, the new head of the Temple of Truth, to tell him what had happened to her, about how the land had settled on her shoulders and then rejected her. She hadn't wanted to tell anyone. Of course, her mother and father hadn't believed her when she'd tried to tell them, hadn't even wanted to see her. Her sister Befery might have believed her, but she'd been called away by her youngest daughter and hadn't talked to Akalina alone. Pamosi hadn't been there—she rarely visited the family anymore, not since marrying that awful husband.

Ghosts didn't breathe, not like the living did. Rosahaptu's breath, though, had always smelled of the lavender sachets that were used to preserve a body after death for the viewing, before the body was burned on a giant, magical pyre.

Wosriufi took one last deep breath of the scented air Akalina had provided before he turned to her. He smelled of young pine wood, burning. Maybe it was from the fires he'd used to keep the VeinHolders at bay.

"The boy must accept the Land," he wheezed at her.

Ghosts generally weren't loud. However, since the death of the LandHolder, they'd fallen completely silent. Even now, Akalina could barely hear Wosriufi clearly. It sounded like words carried on a rushing wind, and not the whispers of ghosts.

Akalina waited for the ghost to tell her more, to tell her *how* to get Yimifut to accept the cold mantle of the Land.

As he'd been able to accurately foresee what was going to happen to Ibitsima and the rest of her house, maybe he had too good of an idea of what would happen after he became LandHolder. Maybe that fate was worse than any other.

"Go to him," Wosriufi commanded. Well, as much as a ghost could command the living. "He needs your guidance."

The will that had held Wosriufi in place abruptly dissipated. Instead of floating to a door or a window and gracefully disappearing through it, the mists that kept the ghost in the air started to dissolve rapidly.

Akalina shivered as she watched Wosriufi melt away, his form losing color and shape, until all that remained was a wet, cold spot in the air.

The rest of the ghosts still stood against the walls of her room. Only now, their eyes followed her with expectation.

"What if I don't go?" Akalina said. She wasn't sure how she would get there. Would anybody go with her? Or would she be forced to traverse an unsettled land alone?

Another ghost strode forward, deliberately heading toward the altar that still had thin trails of smoke rising from it. Sankhue, also one of the older ghosts. She'd been a FarmHolder, nominally in charge of all the farmers in her age. She'd been key at directing them to preserve and save food before a horrendous winter had fallen. Without her guidance, many more would have starved.

Sankhue started to "sip" at the air, building the strength necessary to talk with Akalina.

Would she, too, be dissolved by unseen forces if she did?

"Stop," Akalina said. Sankhue did, turning to stare at Akalina with cold, hard eyes.

The ghosts appeared to be aware of the consequences of talking with the living. Wosriufi had sacrificed himself. Akalina had the feeling that she'd never see him again. Sankhue was obviously prepared to do the same.

Akalina needed to find a way to get to Yimifut and to convince the boy to take the Land into himself.

"I will try," she told the ghosts.

Though no sound came from her silent chorus, the ghosts still indicated they were willing to help her. They appeared to join together, some with well-defined hands, some with mere smoky tendrils. As one, they took a step forward, bobbing and bowing at her.

Some help was better than none.

At least she had an idea of how to get rid of the ghosts haunting her if she failed. Make them speak with her.

Until there were none left.

Chapter Six

HOUSE OF COBALT

KINAKI WENT through the slow pushing of hands from one side to the other, concentrating on his breathing. The air still held the faint tint of smoke, as it had since he'd first joined with Wanho. Many of the CollierHolders practiced with him in the early morning light, the only sound the rustling of their robes, the occasional sliding of their feet. The day was dawning bright and clear, a perfect day for a picnic.

Or to start the next massive assault on the border between his lands and the House of Gold.

Kinaki knew that Wanho thought all exercise was useless. The demon was in complete control of their shared body, growing muscles as necessary.

At first, Kinaki had delighted in his newfound strength, in how he'd started growing taller than all those around him.

It was only after the attack on Ibitsima, less than a week ago, that Kinaki finally started to have second thoughts.

What would have happened if he hadn't accepted Wanho's offer? If he hadn't allowed the demon to bring him back from the dead? Would the demon have taken him anyway?

He believed that would have been the case. He would have been a weaker man as a result.

The form caused Kinaki to pivot with the rest of the warriors, as if battling an enemy on the side. Glancing at his fellow warriors, he could tell the difference between those who'd welcomed a demon, those who'd been taken, and those who would do the bidding of demons without that stain on their soul.

Those without demonic possession shone the brightest, had a clear silver light that burned deep within them. Those who had cooperated with the demons were the next brightest, though they oozed a sickly yellow glow, like infected pus.

The ones who'd been taken barely had any light showing. The silver of their soul was tainted, like a light showing through a cracked, dirty glass. Those warriors also seemed the dullest. They had no wit left, and were best at following orders, not giving them.

Kinaki hadn't realized how many of his men were no longer his, not until that night with Ibitsima.

Today, he'd lead a massive assault against Unnir's lands. Yes, she was weak. However, by dividing up his army, sending half of it to the south, he'd been able to give her a bit of aid, to help her survive his massive onslaught.

At least for a little while.

What Wanho didn't realize was that when Kinaki stretched, or went through the warrior forms, or sometimes even when he ate, Wanho's hold on Kinaki was weakened. Kinaki found himself thinking his own thoughts, uninfluenced by the demon.

Most of the time he was not in control of his opinions. Though he was the one who spoke, the demon subtly dictated what the LandHolder said.

Only during times like these could Kinaki think clearly.

And be terrified by what he'd done.

He'd given Unnir a chance by splitting his armies, by sending a large portion to the south to continue to hold and battle with the barbarians. Wanho didn't really have a good grasp of Kinaki's landsense. He'd thought that any territory Kinaki had acquired to the south would feed him.

Eventually, that land could come under control of the House of Cobalt. But he'd have to place farmers there first, and towns, to awaken it.

That was the problem with the barbarian lands, why they were so difficult to hold onto. The land itself wasn't as aware. It could be brought to life, but that took time.

In the meanwhile, while Unnir would have to face his immense force, she might have a chance. If she was smart, brave, and lucky.

Kinaki wished he had more time to do his warrior form that morning. He had more planning to do, yet another daring gamble to make. One that Wanho could never find out about.

Tomorrow would be another day. Another chance to put things into motion. Kinaki felt his thoughts slide back down, nestled in between the great coils of the demon serpent who curled around his body.

Why was he feeling such darkness? As if a black cloud had gathered over his head? He shook himself, then bowed with the group toward the south, the seat of power.

Kinaki felt the demon and his thoughts swelling within him. He found himself agreeing with Wanho. Yes, today would be a glorious day. Unnir and her puny VeinHolders would fall before him. He would taste the sweetness of her land, consume its power, fill his landsense to the breaking point.

It wouldn't be enough. Nothing would ever be enough. There was not enough power in the land or the underworld for him.

Soon, it would be time to challenge the gods themselves.

Chapter Seven

HOUSE OF GOLD

TORJA BLANCHED when she saw the mass of warriors stretched out before her on the open field. Just past their camp, the border between the House of Gold and the House of Cobalt lay. Today, the warriors would meet for the first time in battle.

Despite the fact that Torja could rarely do auguries or give an accurate foretelling, the VeinHolders still wanted blessings from the Temple of Truth and the God Djediese.

Or rather, from her first, then from the other temples. Starga, the head of the Temple of the Moon, represented the Goddess Morta, she who brought the storms as well as the healing winds afterward. Warriors worshiped her primarily.

She would go last, giving her blessings and rousing the troops.

The sun was just a hand's width above the horizon, the air still chill. Torja and her fellow priestesses and priests stood on a pavilion at the side of the wide meadow, raised so that all could see her. The day was going to be sunny and warm. The air smelled of baked grass still, and the earth churned up by so many feet.

These warriors should be tending their crops, or digging in the mines, not going to fight an impossible battle with creatures from nightmares.

Torja couldn't tell them that, however. Nor could she admit just how blind she and the others in her temple were.

She had to give them hope. It was why Unnir had insisted on completely healing Torja's face, removing all traces of her great ordeal. Her skin was completely smooth, now. The fine hairs of her eyebrows had grown back, as had the brown hair around her face. The only sign that remained was in her green eyes. She couldn't hide the pain she felt there. Few wrinkles marred her skin, but she knew her eyes made her look older than her thirty some years.

Unnir had given strict orders for the Temple of Truth to keep lying.

Torja was determined to do that within limits.

She stepped forward, bowing to the warriors, to those who would give their lives for the House of Gold today.

"I have seen many deaths, today," Torja announced.

The group before her grew still. She hadn't planned on Unnir amplifying her voice so that all could hear her.

She gulped and pressed on.

"I have not foreseen a victory today," she said. She felt the other priests and priestesses beside her on the stage grow still.

She could hear their thoughts pressing in on her—what in the name of the Granite Tombs was she doing?

"There are gold linings to these dark times, though," Torja continued. "There will be great moments of bravery. Great deeds and battles. As well as horrible deaths and crushing defeats."

The warriors before her appeared to sway, uncertain on their feet. Torja felt it with them.

"None of that matters," Torja said firmly. "Instead, I

would have you remember that for every dusk, there is a dawn. For every night, there is a day. We won't get through these battles today or tomorrow, or even next week. But we *will* get through them. The gold of our house will continue to shine, even in the coming darkness. You will be victorious if you hold this in mind. Be true to your house! Be true to your golden selves! Shun the darkness! Keep turning toward the light! And you will win!!!!"

The cheer that followed started softly and grew, a groundswell of support and determination, until all the warriors were shouting at the tops of their lungs, "We will win! We will win! We will win!"

Torja bowed deeply to them. Even without the gift of foresight she knew that many who faced her now were the dead, still walking.

They would make it through this. She believed in her LandHolder. She believed in the land. She believed in the beauty bestowed on the world from the God Djediese.

The demons, headed by the Bandit SlugHolder, could not win. Or even if they did, it would be temporary. Beauty and good earth would rule the day.

Someday.

Chapter Eight

HOUSE OF PEARL

DARIKUTO RESTED at the head of the great army that evening. Gray cloth made up the walls of his tent, like storm clouds on the horizon. He slept alone, both his consort and his wife still safely ensconced back in Yawatan. The cot was ordinary, plain cloth and wood. It looked identical to the other cots the army carried, as well as the blankets and sheets. He had given himself a fluffy pillow, and felt certain that whoever else had needed such comforts had created them for themselves.

Despite the weariness that followed moving such a large number of people through his lands, Darikuto still couldn't sleep. Like a child anticipating either their birthday or one of the grand holidays, he was too excited.

In two days' time, they would arrive in the lands of the House of Crystal. He anticipated nominal resistance from the guards at the border. However, though the group who accompanied him did not contain all of his warriors, he was certain they were sufficient to the task.

Darikuto had not wondered why Chuyoko had left so many of the troops behind. It was obvious to him: taking the

House of Crystal's lands would be as easy as slipping into gentle waves. It would be like coming home. The people there were surely unhappy with no LandHolder. Even a foreign one was likely to be better than living in an unsettled land.

Few ancient books detailed what it was like for a LandHolder to take over another's land. Darikuto's father had found a diary from a LandHolder who'd tried it more than three centuries in the past.

From that slim, hand-lettered volume, Darikuto had gathered the spells necessary to wrestle the control of a foreign land to himself.

The hymns and verses were quite long, and Darikuto wasn't certain if they were actually necessary. There was also a chance that the LandHolder who'd penned the small diary had added all the prayers in order to confuse those who followed after him. The lines pertaining to taking another's land were few, interspersed with unrelated tidbits such as how the field preparation had been going that spring.

None of the LandHolders wanted such a text to exist, while at the same time, they were all secretly fascinated by such a thing. However, as part of the agreement of the peace they'd come to five years previously, they'd committed to destroying what few texts had survived.

This one was still around because its true purpose remained hidden.

Darikuto had dedicated not just weeks but months to memorizing every word so that he could recite the prayers if necessary.

Chances were, the land would welcome him and it wouldn't be necessary.

For a while, Darikuto lay in the darkness on his cot, listening to the sounds of the warriors around him. He envied those who snored with ease.

Guards passed just outside his tent door, an ever vigilant force surrounding him. Not because Chuyoko believed he couldn't take care of himself, but she felt better if she thought she was protecting him somehow.

He still wasn't certain how he was going to reward his most ardent follower. She *believed* in him like no other, not even the head priest of the Temple of Truth, Shimokoro. She would follow all his orders without question or doubt.

In the coming weeks, he may end up relying on that fanaticism.

Darikuto had made other adjustments to The Plan over the past few days. He had originally planned on taking Unnir's lands after the pair of them had defeated Kinaki. However, he wasn't sure that was wise, now. Kinaki was much stronger than Darikuto had anticipated.

The demon who'd possessed him was much stronger. It was as if the demon had been waiting all along for this chance.

So now, Darikuto had a fork in The Plan. After he absorbed the lands of the House of Crystal, he would turn his attention to the House of Gold.

If Unnir was making progress fighting Kinaki, he would join by her side and defeat the demon.

If Unnir was losing her battles, he would attack her. Better for him to hold the lands of the House of Gold than the demons.

It was not time, though, to communicate his intent. For now, it was better that Chuyoko and the others believe that The Plan was still in its original form.

She would follow him regardless. Of that, he was certain.

Chapter Nine

HOUSE OF CRYSTAL

AKALINA CAME STORMING out of her meeting with Menhaptu. She stomped down the hallway. Luckily, no one tried to stop her, so she made it all the way back to her own rooms before she said something stupid and cutting.

That *idiot* priest. Thinking that *she* might be to blame for the corruption of the Chamber of Crystals! He didn't know when the corruption had started. Possibly far before the chamber had declared that she attend the ghost court.

How dare he? Particularly when she had news for him, could tell him who the next LandHolder should have been? How she'd been directed by the ghosts to go convince him?

Akalina had never been close to Menhaptu. Then again, she hadn't been that close to Haptomi, either, when he'd been alive. The older priest had treated her with a cloying sweetness that hadn't sat well with her, had always seemed false, particularly given his general stiff nature.

But surely Menhaptu would have at least *listened* to her when she told him of the Land settling, then rejecting her before going off to find Yimifut.

She hadn't even had a chance to tell him about Wosriufi dying in order to tell her what to do next.

Menhaptu was not going to be any help. That was for damned certain.

Akalina had hoped that Menhaptu would give her a guide or a priest or something to help her on her journey to go see Yimifut, up at Holder Sitre's property. It was one of the northern-most Holds in the land, and butted onto the impassable mountains that demarcated that border of the House of Crystal.

Though Akalina had gone on Promenade with the rest of the LandHolder's family, she still didn't know what to do, where to start. She would need food for the road, though there would be inns along the way. Warm clothes. Coins to pay innkeepers.

Would Akalina's magic still work once she left the palace and the capital Nyati? Would there be enough ghosts to preserve her?

She flung open her wardrobe, then paused. What should she take? She couldn't pack a trunk that someone would magically move between inns and Holds. She would have to find a farmer's rucksack somewhere.

What would her mother say when she found out that Akalina had left?

Good riddance, probably.

Neither her mother nor her father had supported her once they'd discovered she was barren. They had set their hopes on her becoming the next LandHolder. There would be no politically advantageous marriage for her. She'd go into the Temple of Truth, and they'd turn their backs on her. They had made that clear the last time she'd tried to talk with them.

Akalina pulled out shirts, skirts, even warm trousers, piling them all high on her bed.

What should she take? What should she leave? What was she going to do?

"What are you doing?"

At first, Akalina thought that she must have just spoken the words out loud. It took her a moment to look up and see that her sister, Befery, stood just inside the door.

Befery looked as beautiful as always, with the clear blue eyes of their family, long black hair, and pale skin. She wore a rust-colored loose blouse that morning that made her look motherly, as well as a long black, lightweight skirt.

"I have to go find the new LandHolder," Akalina said. She picked up her thickest stockings and put them to the side. "I need to convince him that he must accept the Land."

"I see," Befery said. "And where might you find the next LandHolder?"

"I met him, during the Promenade I went on," Akalina said. She saw no reason to lie. Not as if anyone were going to believe her. "He told me that I was going to be the only one to survive."

"Why do you think he's the next LandHolder?" Befery said. She sounded as though she really wanted to understand. Not, as she had done when they'd been young, to get Akalina to tell her enough so that Befery could tease her.

"After the Land rejected me, it traveled on to him. And he rejected it," Akalina explained. She'd already told this to her family, hadn't she? Or had Befery had to leave early, due to one of her younger children crying, and so had missed that part?

"I see," Befery said.

Akalina had her attention on the skirts in front of her, trying to choose between them, when suddenly Befery was at her side.

"This one," Befery said. "It's lighter. You'll be able to layer clothes underneath, if you need to."

"Thank you," Akalina said. She blinked and looked over at her sister. "Can you get me a farmer's rucksack? Or would you know where I can find one?"

Befery grinned at her. "I'll do better than that. I'll find two."

"I don't understand," Akalina said, confused. How could she carry two rucksacks? Wouldn't that be too heavy for her?

"I'm going with you, idiot," Befery said.

"Oh," Akalina said. She glanced over her shoulder at the ghosts still lining the walls.

Of course, they said nothing. Some help.

"Why?" Akalina said. "Why would you go with me?"

Befery continued to sort the clothes on Akalina's bed into a large pile of what she assumed weren't appropriate travel clothes and a much, much smaller pile of what were.

Akalina reached out and took her sister's hands in hers. The skin was rough, chapped, and raw.

"What have you been doing?" Akalina couldn't help but ask.

Befery shrugged. "Washing the little one's things," she said. "No magic to clean them with."

Up close, Akalina could see how tired Befery was. She had some pale powder under her eyes but it couldn't really hide the dark circles there. Her blue eyes also held a fear that Akalina had never seen before. Like Akalina, Befery had black hair that had a mind of its own and was always escaping whatever pins she tried to tame it with.

Befery smiled at Akalina. "We're the same height, now," she said.

"I'm taller, actually," Akalina said immediately. "But that's not the point. Why do you want to go with me?"

"Someone needs to take care of you," Befery said. "You're obviously not capable of doing it yourself."

"No, really, why do you want to come with me?" Akalina

insisted, not letting her sister turn away even though she looked back at the bed, unwilling to meet Akalina's eye.

"I'm always working here, now," Befery said finally. "The little ones take so much care. And there's no magic now to help."

Akalina snorted. "So, what, you think that crossing an unsettled land with precarious magic is going to be easier?"

Befery finally turned back to look at Akalina directly. "No. It will be different, and just as hard. But you are all alone. Mother and Father won't help. The priests are probably useless as well. Right?"

Akalina nodded grimly. "Yes. Menhaptu wouldn't even listen to me."

"Which means it's just you and me," Befery said firmly.

"What about your little ones?" Akalina said.

"They have their father, who actually loves them and will take good care of them," Befery said, finally smiling again. "You need me more."

Akalina studied her sister for a few more moments. What she said was true. Akalina could use her help. They'd never been close, not as children. Certainly not after Befery had married. There were eight years between them.

But maybe they could get closer on this trip. If they didn't end up killing each other.

"All right," Akalina said. "You may come with me. But we'll need to travel hard and fast, as fast as we can." No one knew for certain, but surely one or another of the other LandHolders had already turned their eye on the "open" lands of the House of Crystal.

If Yimifut didn't take the mantle of the land soon, someone else would.

While many might think that having any LandHolder was better than having none, Akalina had spent too much time listening to Ibitsima and the others in court. It would be a disaster for generations if they allowed it to happen. Particularly Darikuto, who Ibitsima had never trusted.

"You'll see how fast I can move," Befery promised her. "Chasing after little ones keeps you in shape."

After Befery had left, Akalina turned to the ghosts. They still lined her chamber, but maybe, perhaps, instead of just being expectant, they might have hope.

Either that, or they were just thankful that she wasn't going to ask another of them to kill themselves answering her questions.

At least, not yet.

Chapter Ten
HOUSE OF COBALT

WANHO gloried in the battle before him. He'd fought when he'd been in the underworld. Led armies against other demons, huge troops of captured souls, destroying each other so that he might gain a little more land, a few more WarHolders, a touch more respect.

Up in the land of the living, it was all different.

The underworld muted all the senses. So there were no grunts of pain, no screams of terror, no mad cackling of glee as your enemies fell before you. He could smell the fresh dirt dug up by the running of heavy feet, and the rank smell of gore from the living spilling their guts, that was different from anything else he'd ever encountered.

He would have to see if he could recreate that scent somehow, maybe grow a flower that would capture that luscious smell. It would have to bloom only at night, to flavor the dreams of the living who smelled it.

Kinaki complained about the feel of the land around here, how it wasn't as strong so close to the border between the two houses. Wanho couldn't tell the difference, and quite frankly, at first, hadn't thought it was important.

It had made Kinaki uneasy. Wanho tried to assure him that they'd erase the border soon enough. But it was difficult to concentrate when Kinaki was so unsettled. So Wanho had grudgingly agreed to move to the back of the line, to let his troops bear the brunt of the force.

He strode back and forth behind the lines, using his magic to get a sense of the battle. Before him, two large armies fought, masses of men and women. Past that, the damned golden curtain/barrier between the two lands still stood. It looked like a waterfall of piss, but it was one he couldn't approach or breach.

Wanho yearned to be out there with the warriors, slicing bodies in two with his mighty sword, tearing heads off with his mighty strength, maybe even feasting on the blood of the living.

For now, he tried to see the bigger picture, as Kinaki advised.

Unnir had been smarter than either Kinaki or Wanho had originally given her credit for. She'd placed her people on the wrong side of the barrier, having them make their stand on the House of Cobalt's lands.

At first, Wanho (and Kinaki) had assumed that was a mistake on her part. Why endanger her people by allowing them to leave their land?

But they, too, were less affected by the lands in the House of Cobalt so close to the border. They were strong enough in their magic (and their brute force) to keep Wanho's troops away from that golden flowing piss curtain that shimmered just behind them.

Which made it impossible for Wanho's WarHolders to overwhelm the House of Gold's defenses.

It was far too easy for her warriors to just step back, go behind the curtain, rejuvenate themselves, then go out into battle again.

Frustrated, Wanho had directed all his efforts at one small space along the border, trying to overwhelm Unnir's force there.

In the second day of fighting, he still had yet to see any results.

They outnumbered Unnir's forces. She should have fallen. He'd promised his WarHolders that they'd be feasting on her warriors by now.

Instead, despite the fierce battles, Unnir's forces seemed undefeatable. The small force was well defended with superior magical armor and tactics.

It couldn't be Unnir directing her troops. It had to be someone in her retinue who was the brains behind their brilliant strategies. And there was no way of getting a spy back there, or an assassin.

Maybe if Wanho had more troops…he still wasn't sure about Kinaki's strategy to split their forces, send half of them down south to the barbarians and only have a portion here.

We need more warriors, Wanho whispered at Kinaki.

"Maybe," Kinaki said after examining their ragged line again. They just couldn't push through to the curtain, damn it! Wanho was certain they could overwhelm it once they actually reached it.

"Or maybe we need to be less straightforward," Kinaki added after a moment. He turned to one of the CollierHolders who attended him, who carried messages to the WarHolders. "Tell me, how fast could we get warriors up and down the line? Small, discrete groups attacking all along the border?"

The warrior woman thought. "Half a day. Or better, we pull back earlier this evening, supposedly disgruntled, then we place the warriors along the border all through the night. Some are sure to make it through, particularly if they find a spot that isn't well defended."

What is the point? Wanho asked petulantly. So what if one or two warriors made it into the House of Gold lands?

"How would they signal success?" Kinaki asked. "So that we might quickly amass a force there?"

"Nightly runners?" the warrior proposed. In a place where their landsense didn't work well, sending messengers up and down the line would be a good way to ascertain when someone had made it across the border.

"It would be a longer strategy," Kinaki mused out loud.

Wanho appreciated that Kinaki did this for him, spoke his thoughts so that the demon could follow.

"A small group infiltrates the House of Gold. Or several. We pick the weakest point and cross over with a larger group. Or possibly many smaller groups. Then, we hit them from behind their precious border in a coordinated attack. They'll have to pull warriors back from the line, here. Once they do that, we rush forward and overwhelm that damned curtain," Kinaki said.

Wanho marveled once again at the trickiness of the living. A demon would never have come up with such a strategy. He would have stayed focused on this point, battling and losing warriors until he'd been forced to give up.

This plan was much more elegant and subtle than that. It would take time, yes. Wanho wasn't known for his patience.

But he'd restrain his impatience. Let the living have their strategies and their delays.

Soon enough, he'd have a new land to consume. New power to draw on.

Maybe soon he'd have enough strength to pull away from the anchor of the living who held him back.

Yes. Soon.

Chapter Eleven

HOUSE OF GOLD

EMIL COLLAPSED in a weary heap on his camp chair. He still wore his bloodied, stained armor from that day's battle. He'd been slaughtering demons since sunup. He stank, every muscle hurt, he'd used more magic that day than he had in the past week and so even his soul was weary.

Tomorrow, he would have to get up and do it all again.

He was too tired to use magic to take off the armor pieces he wore. Instead, he forced his thick, fumbling fingers to push blood-soaked leather straps through their buckles, sliding first his bracers then his greaves to the floor. He kicked off his boots, which finally made him to find a small breeze to blow the stench away as he flexed and curled his aching toes.

Slowly, he stripped himself of his metal suit. It was magically lightweight and strong. Despite the pounding he'd taken, it didn't have a single dent in it. He was too tired to clean it now, but in the morning, he'd use his magic to wash away all the dirt, gore, and grime, and it would look brand new, golden and green, sleek and shiny.

He was just too damned tired to anything other than to leave it in a heap on the floor.

Fortunately, someone had seen to his tent, and had left a bottle of wine on the table with two glasses. He wasn't expecting company, but he still used the glass and didn't just drink straight from the bottle.

He'd spent part of the afternoon and evening meeting with the other VeinHolders, discussing strategies, what had worked against the demons (very little) and what hadn't (far too much). He'd eaten what food he could.

Now, he was going to pretend that all was normal in his world, at least for the few moments he could before he collapsed into sleep. Sip a glass of damned good wine, stretch his limbs out, pretend that there was a hearth over there with nicely warmed rocks and perhaps a good book for him to read. Instead of gray canvas walls, a grass-covered floor, and an empty stand on which to hang his armor.

"May I join you?"

Emil blinked slowly. He hadn't heard Vide come in. Not that his younger brother would have knocked or anything.

"Don't have the strength to stop you," Emil said heavily.

Vide took two steps closer to where Emil was sprawled out on his chair. "I would leave if you told me to," Vide said seriously.

"Naw, come. Sit," Emil said. "Just don't expect sparkling conversation."

"I never do, not from you, dear brother," Vide said, just a hint of his regular wit returning.

Emil felt the first smile of the day cross his face. "How have you been?" he said after a moment.

Vide didn't look as exhausted as Emil. Then again, he always hid everything better. Vide was pale though, much more pale than usual. His dark hair was pulled back tightly, giving his thin face more severe angles. Large blue eyes gazed out, his expression more serene and less mocking. He wore the same sort of lounging clothes that Emil wore, loose shirt and trousers, though his were a lot cleaner.

"I've been fine," Vide said, pouring himself a glass of wine. "I've been working on strategies for the VeinHolders and the LandHolder. Since we have no foretelling, we need to out-think our enemy."

Emil nodded. He'd suspected that had been what Vide had been up to.

There weren't many who were smarter than Vide, and that included the LandHolder. At least she'd had the sense to see that and to put that brain of his to work.

While Emil was being used for his brawn.

"How are you?" Vide said. "You should really get a servant in here to clean this up," he added, his gesture taking in the tent as well as the heaped armor.

Emil grimaced. "They have enough to do. They don't need to take care of me when I'm perfectly capable of taking care of myself."

The real reason was because of the looks Emil had first gotten when he'd joined the ranks of the fighters. Everyone was far too polite to say anything to him. But no one expected much from him.

At least, not at first.

He had been groomed by his father to take over the land, if it hadn't chosen his cousin. He might not have joined the warriors every morning doing their drills and their stretches. He still spent time every day training.

Few knew that, though.

After the first day, the other VeinHolders had started to listen to Emil when he suggested things. His title of VeinHolder was merely honorary. Only now, he'd been accepted into the ranks of the warriors.

Vide narrowed his eyes at Emil. "Fine, then." He waved

his hand. Emil's suit was suddenly hanging where it belonged, thoroughly cleaned. Emil felt better as well, as if the land had wrapped itself around him and was now cushioning him, supporting every aching muscle.

"Thank you," Emil said. "I appreciate it." He would have gotten to it sooner or later. He had appearances to maintain, after all.

Vide opened his mouth then shut it again. He gave a rueful smile and shook his head. "What is happening to us, dear brother? I'm actually using my wits to their fullest extent. And you—rumor has it that you're turning into an actual leader."

Emil snorted. "I know, right? Since when did I become a leader of men? And not just a shouter of orders?" He sobered at the thought. "I don't think anyone could have foreseen this."

Vide took a sip of his wine, then nodded. "Torja has a wild idea about how Kinaki stole all of our foresight. She has the most impossible tale of a Bandit SlugHolder who stole her fletche."

Emil shrugged. He'd never dealt with auguries except when he needed to. A man made his own fate, or at least that was what their father, Yudur, had maintained.

He was determined to make his a good one.

"But I do think she's on to something. The House of Crystal said their ghosts had grown scarce, as they have in all the lands. There's some connection between the ghosts and foretelling that we've never pursued before," Vide said.

"I will leave that in your capable hands," Emil said. He gave a jaw-cracking yawn. He couldn't help it.

Vide immediately stood up. "I'm sorry to have been keeping you from your much-needed rest."

Emil sighed and nodded. He knew that Vide hadn't

meant the words as snottily as they had come out. That was just Vide's way.

"Sorry," Emil said as he rose, swaying, to his feet.

Suddenly Vide was right there, one arm wrapped around Emil's waist, the other tugging Emil's arm over Vide's shoulders.

"Come on," Vide said, using a chiding voice that one generally reserved for a three-year-old. "Since you don't have the sense to get to your cot on your own."

Emil didn't mean to put as much weight on Vide as he did. But he couldn't help it. The room was spinning and dark around the edges.

He was just so tired.

"I know you're tired," Vide said in one of the gentlest voices Emil had ever heard. "But I'm not a great oaf such as you. You need to shuffle your feet a little so I can get you to bed."

Emil grinned and tried to do as his brother had asked.

Slowly, one step at a time, they walked the few feet across the grass floor of the small tent to the side, where Emil collapsed onto the cot there.

"Sweet dreams, dear brother," Vide said softly as he drew the covers up over Emil. "Now rest. Rest deeply. Heal yourself so that you'll be ready for the morrow."

Emil nodded.

Surely he imagined the last words Vide whispered. "You better keep yourself well, you great galoot. I can't do this without you."

But when he opened his eyes, Vide was long gone and the dawn was already approaching.

Time for a new day. A new battle, not just with the demons, but to keep the hopelessness away.

Chapter Twelve

HOUSE OF PEARL

BENITOYO IGNORED the sound of slithering that he heard drifting in from his open windows. He kept his attention focused on the letter he was writing to his wife, and not the smell of rotten meat that seeped in sometimes, the scent of decay and smoke that was everywhere, the feeling that the floors shifted sometimes when he walked on them.

His rooms were the same as always: a comfortable sitting room in the front where he could greet and entertain a half dozen people comfortably; and the small room in the back with a wardrobe in the corner and a bed piled high with a soft, well-stuffed mattress.

He had the feeling that it all was different, now. A black film appeared to cover the window, whether it was open or not. It wasn't just the smells, but the taste of everything that had gone off.

And the noises—best to ignore those. Particularly like now, when he thought he heard the slithering of a thousand snakes, or the squelching sound of wet maggots brushing against one another in their heaping barrels.

Benitoyo's rooms faced the kitchens of the palace. It had been ideal, the perfect location for him to slip the poison that Shimokoro had given him into Kinaki's salt.

Just a little bit every day had brought the LandHolder low.

Now, Benitoyo had considered asking to be changed to a different set of rooms. However, he wasn't certain that anywhere else would actually be better. It might be worse in some ways, being placed higher in the palace, so that he no longer had a second escape route out of his rooms.

Benitoyo had heard the rumors that the LandHolder was possessed by a demon from the underworld. He believed it, despite how little Shimokoro would tell him.

He also believed others when they told him that the land itself was now possessed. Benitoyo didn't have a strong landsense. It was one of the reasons why he could be a merchant, here in Jinyi, so far away from the House of Pearl's lands.

Few could see clearly what exactly the palace had turned into. Benitoyo found someone who said she was a mystic, who claimed that she used the old fashioned ways of producing visions.

She came to his rooms one night, and danced like a swirling wind, circling hard and fast, finally falling into an exhausted heap and reeling off prophecy and nonsense.

It was up to Benitoyo to separate the two. He'd thought long and hard about the walls covered in heaving vines, the black pits in the streets, the demons everywhere, finally deciding that he believed all of it. Even the less believable parts had to be the truth, such as the pens holding ghosts in the back of the palace and the miasma that the flowers exuded, dulling the senses and stopping people from questioning why.

Benitoyo hadn't tried going back to the lands of the House of Pearl, though he knew that many in the city had fled when Ibitsima had been killed. Half the stalls in the market were empty.

War brought opportunities, however. Benitoyo continued to supply the warriors and the palace with goods from his warehouses, despite the bribes he now had to pay guards to keep his storehouses safe.

In many ways, the world had gone mad.

Benitoyo continued to pen daily letters to his wife, Ozukshi, who was still in Yawatan, the capital of the House of Pearl. He had no idea how many of them would arrive. He assumed that at least some of them would. He needed to assure his family that he was still alive, that they shouldn't start the plans to blackmail Darikuto should Benitoyo meet with a suspicious end.

With every letter, Benitoyo tried to slip in a little more of the actual news of things that were happening in the palace. He hoped that Ozukshi was good enough at reading between the lines that she'd be able to grasp his meaning without him spelling everything out.

She was smarter than he, after all. As well as far more stubborn. She'd been the one who'd encouraged him to become a spy in the first place. She'd also ensured that their children practiced their landsense, certain that they would be able to acquire and Hold a large piece of the land.

Officially, Benitoyo was not the only supplier for the army. Unofficially, through a series of backroom deals and handshake bargains, quite a few of the other suppliers also worked for him. So Benitoyo had a better idea than any other merchant of just what was happening with the warriors.

He had only learned that morning that the warriors had

been split, that a very large portion of the army, along with both WarHolders and CollierHolders, had not gone to attack the border between the two lands, but instead, had been sent south.

Was Kinaki really going to maintain two fronts? That seemed idiotic to Benitoyo. Sure, Kinaki needed to leave some level of guards along the southern border, so the barbarians didn't realize that the LandHolder's attention had turned elsewhere.

Yet, it seemed as though Kinaki was committed to expanding in both directions.

Why?

Was he that arrogant? Or was it the demon controlling him?

It was news that Darikuto needed, though. When he came to attack the House of Cobalt, he had to be prepared for a second army to come marching out of the south ready to defend their land.

However, it wasn't news that Benitoyo felt comfortable just telling his wife. He needed to couch it carefully and let her read between the lines, to get a message to Darikuto or Shimokoro.

I have had a successful summer so far, supplying the mighty warriors here, Benitoyo wrote. *I've been less successful finding delivery carts. Supplies need to go everywhere! To the north, to the south! I'm sure if you were here, you would find the perfect solution for my troubles.*

Benitoyo paused and smiled. Hopefully that would be enough of a hint, at least to set Ozukshi asking the right questions.

He went on to write about how he was finally losing weight, as the freshest of everything had to go to the army. (While the first part was true, the second wasn't—the worst of the rotten food actually went to the demons. However, all the food tasted off these days, and Benitoyo wasn't eating as much as a result.)

He also wrote about how he missed her (which was true) as well as their children and grandchildren.

A loud thump from outside made him glance up. There were two cooks outside of the kitchen, standing in the courtyard. One of the cooks had just hit the other with a heavy frying pan. The other cook just laughed.

The fear on the first cook's face went straight to Benitoyo's soul.

One was human. The other…was not.

He took a swig of the bottle of wine that was now constantly open on his desk. He told himself again that he'd done the right thing. If he hadn't done it, Shimokoro would have found someone else. Benitoyo's family wouldn't be as well off as they were now. He wouldn't have the contracts that he had, and money wouldn't be pouring into the family coffers.

The guilt still overwhelmed him some nights.

Ozukshi would tell him that he hadn't done anything shameful. He'd helped their house. Their children, and their grandchildren, would be much richer as a result.

The shame would remain with him, not be transferred to them. Only he would be denied the Golden Lands, of that, he was certain.

He finished off the letter promising to return soon. There was a delivery service in the city center that he used, that would get the letter to Yawatan. They'd originally used messengers. Benitoyo wondered if all correspondence between the two lands was now being sent magically, somehow.

It didn't matter. He still sent his letter. It was part of what he did to assuage his soul.

It was also why he stayed there, at the palace, with the

rotten meat, the constant fear, and the writhing walls that he saw only in his nightmares—he was partly responsible for this state of affairs. It was only right that he stayed and lived with it.

Chapter Thirteen
HOUSE OF CRYSTAL

BEFERY WASN'T sure what to expect once she and Akalina had left the capital city of Nyati, through the northern gate, and headed into the countryside. Would the fields be swarming with vermin and bugs? Would the ground no longer be solid, but undulate like waves? Would the sky be split, half sunny, half stormy?

She had to admit she was a little disappointed that everything seemed, well, normal. The road they traveled along followed the edge of a wide field. Slight ruts on either side of the gravel-covered road had been carved by heavily laden carts taking food into the market in the city. Summer wheat and other grains filled the flat valley to the horizons, as well as the occasional herds of cows or sheep. The sun shone down brightly, making Befery glad that she'd insisted on large straw hats for both of them.

"What?" Akalina finally asked when it appeared that Befery had paused to wonder.

"This isn't how I expected it to be," Befery admitted.

Akalina appeared to understand what Befery meant.

"Don't worry. The land grows a lot wilder the further we get from the city or any towns."

"How do you know that?" Befery asked as they started walking again.

They both wore good boots, long skirts, and long-sleeved shirts. Not because it was cold, but to protect them from the bright sunlight. Befery didn't have confidence that her magic would keep her pale skin from burning, not during these times. Their rucksacks were made out of light-weight wooden frames, with canvas stretched over them. She'd packed both of them, not trusting Akalina to be sensible.

Akalina shrugged. She did that a lot. It was very annoying. Befery would have to remember to train her girls to not answer in that fashion.

"Is it your landsense that's telling you that?" Befery persisted. "How far away the chaos is?"

"It's some of that," Akalina said, nodding. "It's also the presence of the ghosts. They feel wild up ahead."

"What does that even mean?" Befery said, alarmed. She'd been prepared to deal with an unsettled land and unpredictable magic, not with untamed ghosts.

"I don't know," Akalina said, sounding a bit cross. "We haven't met them yet. I can only tell you what I feel, not anything that I know."

"I see," Befery said.

They walked for a while in silence, when a dark forest suddenly loomed in front of them.

"Where did that come from?" Befery asked. There weren't any forests close to the capital city.

"It's the Angkhar Forest," Akalina said, as if she expected Befery to know that.

"But that's over a day's travel away from Nyati!" Befery said. "We've only walked a few hours."

"Oh," Akalina said, looking sheepish. "I thought you realized I was helping us move faster."

"What do you mean?" Befery said, alarmed. How strong was her little sister's magic?

"While we're in a place that's more stable, I thought it would be best for us to move as fast as we could," Akalina explained. "When I was on Promenade, the LandHolder would move the entire retinue along quickly, so that one step is actually more like ten or twenty."

"I see," Befery said, though she didn't. "And how soon before we reach somewhere that's less stable?"

Akalina thought for a moment. Befery found it fascinating how her sister seemed to turn in on herself, her sight focused inward. Was she consulting with her ghosts, now? She did that a lot in the palace, looking over Befery's shoulder to the ghosts she assumed had been in Akalina's room.

"Past the forest is less stable," Akalina said eventually, her eyes refocusing on what was around her.

"Then let's make it through the woods as quickly as possible," Befery said. She reached out and squeezed her sister's cold hand, then let it go.

That was one thing that had changed about Akalina over the years. She'd never been a demonstrative child, had never climbed up onto Mother or Father's lap demanding attention and hugs. Befery had done that, as had Pamosi. Instead, Akalina kept to herself, always on the sidelines of the rest of the family.

Befery had to admit that when she'd been younger and thoughtless, she'd sometimes pretended that Akalina didn't exist, that she was just a ghost.

Now, her sister was even less in the present day. She'd been infected by her ghosts, and Befery suspected she lived partly in their world.

Akalina didn't see how dark the forest before them was, didn't hear the creaking limbs or feel the cold winds.

The forest was as haunted as the ghost court back in the city.

Hopefully the ghosts here were friendly.

BEFERY NOTICED the cold of the forest first. It was as if a wind directly from the snow-covered mountains had rushed at her, sinking deep under her skin, into her bones. Then the light, or the lack of it. It was so much darker here under the canopy of trees. Not just dim, but gloomy. She hadn't noticed the birds in the fields, not until she could no longer hear them. Instead, it was a stilted silence, like someone holding their breath afraid to be caught. At least the smell was nice, like pine trees and rich soil.

Akalina was still moving them along faster. It was easier here for Befery to tell the difference, as the trees blurred by in a strange fashion that hadn't been apparent when they'd been surrounded by fields. The road among the trees was rockier and more pitted, the gravel not as smooth.

Would farmers going to market through these woods have to use a lot of magic to move their carts along? That was all Befery could think of.

The trees around them rustled in a wind she couldn't feel.

Akalina abruptly stopped. Befery noticed when she took a few heavy steps on her own, her sister no longer moving them along.

"What is it?" Befery asked, looking back.

Akalina's pale face had grown white. She gulped visibly.

"The land here is less tame than I thought," Akalina said quietly. "It doesn't like us being here."

"Then let's get out of here quickly, shall we?" Befery said. She walked back to where her sister still stood, frozen.

"I'm not sure how," Akalina whispered. Her eyes darted between the rough tree trunks, following ghosts Befery couldn't see.

"We just follow the road," Befery said soothingly. She took Akalina's cold hand in hers and tugged. "Just like this."

Akalina stumbled forward. She gasped but kept walking.

They moved a lot more slowly now that they weren't using magic. Befery could tell. Her pack felt heavier as well.

But the road was obvious in front of them, a wide patch between the tree trunks. Bramble gathered to the sides of it. Occasionally, Befery heard small animals rustling in the undergrowth.

After a while, Akalina whispered, "The trees are moving."

"No, they're not," Befery said firmly. "They are staying put, exactly where they're supposed to be," she added, glaring at them as she kept walking. "Stay put," she said, in her best "mom" voice.

At least Akalina stopped dragging her feet. "You'll just order them to behave?" she asked.

"And why shouldn't I?" Befery said. She kept hold of her sister's ice-cold hand, trying to warm it in her own. "They should know enough to listen to their mother."

Akalina giggled. "They've never had a mother," she said, "but they're curious about you."

"Good," Befery said. The trees had moved in, Befery could tell. Instead of bushes and ferns, tree trunks now lined the edges of the road, looming in over them. The branches had lowered as well, not quite brushing against the tops of their straw hats, but getting closer, ready to snatch at them.

The air turned icy the further they walked into the forest. The dim light shrank, as if the sun hidden above them was further obscured by clouds. Rustling sounds grew, the trees talking to themselves. The smell of mulch was all around them, as if the ground nearby had just been plowed.

Or something had been ripped out of the earth, like roots being lifted up so the trees could shuffle forward.

"There are ghosts here, too," Akalina said quietly.

"Of course there are," Befery said. "There are ghosts everywhere." Her heart pounded hard. She felt it in her temples, where her hat rested on her head. Her own hands were growing clammy with the cold, so she tucked her sister's hand in the crook of her elbow, pressing the icy flesh against her torso.

The road remained true, despite the growing dimness all around them. Befery kept them walking at a steady pace, determined to not stop or trip.

Falling off the road into the woods would be devastating. The roots would wrap around them, pull them under the earth, swallow them up whole.

Akalina shook her head. "How can you be so calm?"

Befery gave a rueful laugh. "I'm not calm, not really," she assured her younger sister. "But when you have people relying on you, you make it appear so." Befery wasn't sure why she felt the need to tell Akalina the truth. Maybe so she would learn something.

"All right," Akalina said after a few more moments. "The land is starting to change," she whispered.

"Growing less angry, perhaps?" Befery asked hopefully, though she knew that wasn't going to be the case. The forest didn't like them in here. She could tell that, now.

Her own landsense had increased while she'd been under the trees. It almost felt normal, the earth supporting her. She could tell how far they were away from Nyati for the first time. They'd traveled a good distance their first morning, much farther than she'd imagined.

And she also sensed that just ahead, the land was more open. Still angry, but less focused. More unsettled.

Befery felt Akalina's shrug. She rolled her eyes but didn't say anything.

Really, that was something else she was going to have to teach her sister at some point, to actually respond when someone asked you a question.

For a moment, Befery thought she saw light. Were they reaching the end of the forest? It appeared brighter, just past this section of trees.

Harsh winds rushed past them, blowing from behind. Befery staggered but didn't drop Akalina's hand.

When she looked around again, the light in front of them had faded.

Instead of the end of the trail, a large bramble stood in front of them, blocking the way. It was formed out of cruel, twisted thorns, and easily taller than a tall man. Roots suddenly ran across the road. They grew quickly, from small ropes to knee-height. The smell of mulch increased, as well as the scent of new leaves, bright and green.

Akalina and Befery stopped.

How were they going to get through that?

"The trees want us to turn around," Akalina said quietly.

"No," Befery said. She lifted her chin and glared around her, defiant. "They want to bury us."

"That too," Akalina had to admit.

"They will let us pass," Befery said firmly. She stomped her foot on the road, ignoring the fact that the wind that replied carried the sound of faint laughter.

"Why should it?" Akalina asked, sounding genuinely curious.

Befery pulled on her landsense. Through that, she pulled up a dancing spark into the palm of her hand.

"Because otherwise Mama's going to punish you," she said, using her best "mom" voice again.

Akalina blinked and seemed surprised.

"You will behave," Befery ordered. "We are going through that bramble now."

She took a deliberate step forward, then had to tug on Akalina to get her to follow.

Harsh, cold winds buffeted them from the side. Befery nearly laughed at the forest's attempt to blow out the flame she carried.

The woods had a sense of the land, but not the will to use it. Not like people did.

Befery took another step forward. Then a third.

The roots in front of her feet started to melt away, flowing to the side. They stayed on the road though, not disappearing fully under the trees, a warning to anyone who tried to follow.

Befery was surprised that the road had lasted as long as it had, given how the forest really felt about people.

As they neared the thorny hedge, Befery saw the center of it start to clear slowly, reluctantly, like a grudging two-year-old putting away her toys.

Befery stomped her foot and caused the flame in the center of her palm to spark higher.

Eyes reflected out at them from the edges of the woods. Some were animals, while others she felt were the spirits of the forest.

Akalina just focused forward. For the first time, Befery felt a warmth coming from her sister, where her hand was tucked into her elbow.

Befery's sense of the land expanded. She could tell that just past the edge of the woods the land was different.

Too bad it was just going to have to accept them passing.

The hedge continued to part, until there was a wide enough breach for the pair of them to cross through.

"And don't even think about snagging my skirt when we pass," Befery warned.

Akalina snorted quietly but didn't say anything.

The hedge was thicker than Befery had assumed—at least the width of her arms outstretched. The way the vines and branches continued to twist and twine around each other was fascinating as well as dreadful. The smell of decay struck her as they passed, as if they were stepping through a drowned, rotting field.

The forest was seeking its rotten heart, in order to find the will to combat the people here.

Finally, the sisters passed beyond the hedge, and the edge of the forest itself.

The road disappeared. It had been swallowed by wild fields on either side.

Akalina and Befery looked at each other briefly before they started moving forward again. Finally, they could start moving fast again. Akalina aided their steps with her magic.

Befery glanced back at the woods. It seemed like a black, ominous cloud on the horizon behind her. Even at a distance, she still felt the cold emanating from it.

While ahead of her was a wide field with nothing but grasses filling it. No landmarks. No farms. No road.

Without her own landsense, she'd be lost in a sea of wheat, the green tufts growing up past her knees.

Where were they going? Would there be a town up ahead? She couldn't tell. Her landsense had shrunk down again.

Befery had to trust that Akalina would get them through the next part of their journey.

She was only along for the ride, at least for now.

Chapter Fourteen

HOUSE OF COBALT

SUNLI FOUND he could see much with his new vision, granted to him by the demon Belam. Not just the truth of the palace—with the horrible pits in the roads and the seething walls covered in living vines—but also to see what lay in the hearts of men and women.

He had developed a new routine since that first day: rising early, before the dawn. Walking to the main market, through the empty streets. Even in the middle of the day less than half the stalls were open. People were staying at home, afraid of what might become of them if they went out.

The truth of the merchants shone more clearly in the dim light: the silver-clean souls of those who were still pure, who were just trying to make an honest living; the putrid yellow pus of those who'd cooperated with the demons; and those who'd been taken, the silver of their soul sullied and shaded by cracked, black spiderwebs.

Despite how often Sunli looked in the mirror, he could not see his own soul. He suspected that since he'd cooperated, his soul would be filled with sickening yellow.

It was equally obvious which stalls now catered to the

demons in human form, those with the meat that was green and covered in maggots, or the rotten fruit and vegetables, or even the soured wine and beer.

After strolling through the market, noting the slowly gaining majority of the corrupted, he would walk to the main courtyard of the palace, where the king and his warriors did their morning stretches.

It had shocked him that first day, to see Kinaki entrapped in a serpent's coils, the forked tongue constantly whispering lies and corrupting the man.

Sunli had nearly turned away and left, vowing never to return.

However, as he watched, he noted how the LandHolder's demon appeared to nod off while Kinaki did his morning exercises, how Kinaki's face changed and became filled with regret.

There had to be something that Sunli could do to help his LandHolder, to aid the House of Cobalt.

The second day, Sunli tried to signal to Kinaki that he saw, that he was there to help. The LandHolder smiled, a sincerely happy look. He nodded, indicating he'd understood.

But that was it.

The third day, while Sunli watched, Kinaki seemed to miss a step in the form. Instead of holding an imagined ball of energy between his hands, he turned the top arm and rested it against the bottom one. Just for a moment, he cradled something in his arms, something precious from the look on his face.

Then he shot a hard look at Sunli before continuing the rest of the form.

It was obviously meant as some sort of signal. But of what? What would Kinaki cradle that way?

There was no augury for Sunli, nothing to guide him.

Whatever it was, Kinaki expected him to help here, in Jinyi, as Kinaki, the CollierHolders, and the WarHolders went off to break through the barriers set up at the border of the House of Gold, to consume and corrupt that land as well.

But what was he supposed to do?

Normally, the heads of the four temples would travel with the army, to bless the warriors before their battles. Though not all the warriors were corrupted, enough were that they didn't want or need the blessings of the gods.

So Sunli remained in Jinyi, with the others.

Thankfully, none of them could see his corruption. Though he had to wonder sometimes what they would see. Belam didn't try to interfere with Sunli's daily life. The demon only spoke when Sunli asked a question, needing clarification of what he was seeing.

Belam had commented that Sunli's soul was stronger than he'd expected it to be.

Was that because Sunli had only asked to see? He hadn't asked for power or wealth. Just clarifying sight. And that was so that he could help. While he may have gotten caught up in the minutia of things, he now saw how unimportant that was. Instead, he needed to focus on leading.

However one did that.

Every afternoon, Sunli had taken to trying to soothe the fears and rage of those who remained in the city. Only those with a pure soul sought him out. That they continued to do so, even with his own corruption, astonished him.

What was it they saw? Besides a failed priest fumbling along the best he could?

A few days after the troops had left the city, Sunli had a surprise visit from Lijun, Kinaki's daughter. She'd always been fond of the Temple of Truth. Sunli had sometimes thought she might have an inappropriate crush on Belam.

He received her in a private visitation room, behind the

main altar for the God Djediese. The room was painted a soothing sage green, while the wooden floors had been stained a dark brown. It was almost like being in the forest. There was no real window cut into any of the walls. Instead, a painted window took up almost one entire wall with the view of a delightful garden in bright sunlight, filled with colorful flowers, brilliant bees and butterflies flitting from one flower to the next, a darker forest off in the distance.

The room was free of the damned pots and plants that had taken over so much of the palace. Removing them had been one of the first things that Sunli had gotten rid of throughout the entire temple.

Sunli loved the simplicity of the room, how it warmed his heart. Even Belam appeared soothed here.

However, the room now also had the feel of an ancient relic, a picture looking back into simpler times.

Would they ever be able to return to such a time? Could the land ever be cleansed from the corruption of the demons?

Lijun still wore the true cobalt blue of her house, a beautiful robe with geometric patterns stitched in white. An equally white belt held the robe closed, showing off her dainty figure. Her straw sandals showed wear—maybe she hadn't been able to avoid the pits in the road that only those touched by the demons saw.

"My dear, it's so good to see you," Sunli said. He'd placed plain pillows on the floor for them to sit on, and had a low table with tea already waiting. The pillows had no design on them on purpose, no embroidery that corruption could thread together.

Lijun smiled wanly at him. Her normally ruddy face was pale. Fear lurked at the back of her brown eyes. She wore her black hair bound tightly, the long braid reaching the middle of her back. She was young, only in her twenties, but she moved as though she were ancient.

Sunli offered her his elbow. She leaned on him as she took the few steps into the room, then collapsed onto the pillow.

"Oh, Sunli, it's so good of you to see me," Lijun started off. "We're all so lost these days. This war! The way things have changed."

"I know, my dear, I know," Sunli said. He poured them both a fragrant cup of mint tea. He'd gotten rid of all of the floral teas that he used to drink. The clear smell of the mint seemed to help his vision as well.

"Thank you," Lijun said, taking the cup and sipping gratefully. "And thank you for keeping this space clean."

Sunli wasn't sure exactly what she meant. He'd always seen to the little details, such as making sure that there was no dust in his office, that the floors were spotless.

"And the mint is so refreshing," Lijun continued. "So much better than, say chrysanthemum." She shot him an expectant look.

"Yes, the flowers used for tea don't seem to suit me anymore," Sunli said cautiously, knowing that since Kinaki had declared himself the Flower LandHolder, he was treading on dangerously slippery shale.

"Exactly!" Lijun said. "And there are no flowers or plants in here, either. Just those," she said, indicating the painting.

"It was too stuffy with all that live vegetation," Sunli said, again knowing that he was going directly against the LandHolder's wishes. Or rather, his demon's wishes. "And it was always…dirty." He didn't want to use the word corrupted. He still needed to ascertain what exactly Lijun was hinting at.

"Dirty is one word for it," Lijun said dryly. She took a sip of her tea and they sat in silence for a few moments while she obviously collected her thoughts. Finally, she appeared to come to a decision and nodded. "My brother and our cousins went on Promenade earlier this spring. What we saw disturbed us."

"I remember," Sunli said. He knew that the children of the LandHolder had brought news back of how everyone was having difficulty with augury, as well as how the ghosts had changed.

He hadn't listened. He'd instead believed the LandHolder who'd hinted that perhaps his children were jealous of his position, and needed to be shown their place. He'd set them to doing menial tasks, far away from the capital, out of the way and unable to influence others.

"I also recall that you were working with one of the distant Holders," Sunli said cautiously.

It had been a show of how much the pair of them were in disgrace, being sent far away from the capital during the annual festival, when all the other houses came to visit the House of Cobalt. They should have been there, meeting with their counterparts in the other houses.

"Both I and my brother Chaotu were sent away," Lijun said. "I returned just before…just before Ibitsima was killed."

"Did your brother return with you?" Sunli asked.

"He is in hiding," Lijun said, her tone bleak. "For his own safety."

"He is—oh," Sunli said, putting the pieces together.

The children of the LandHolder had been making things difficult since they'd returned from Promenade. They'd been vocal in their opposition to all the greenery in the palace, had stopped eating meals with the LandHolder, and had expressed concern about all the CollierHolders as well as the WarHolders gathering.

If Chaotu was in hiding for his own safety, that meant that Kinaki had sent guards after him. Demons, probably with instructions to make Chaotu's death appear to have been an accident.

"I'm sorry," Sunli said gently. "It wasn't your father," he added quietly.

"My father no longer exists," Lijun said bitterly.

"He does," Sunli said. He suddenly remembered the message that Kinaki had sent to Sunli the day before, how he'd cradled something in his arms.

Something like a child. One of his babies.

Lijun didn't reply, but Sunli knew that she didn't believe him.

As clear as an augury, Sunli understood what he needed to do.

"I assume you know where your brother is, or that you can get in contact with him," Sunli said.

Lijun gave a cautious nod.

"We must get him, and you, out of here," Sunli said decisively.

Again, that cautious nod.

"You will claim asylum at the House of Gold," he said plainly. "I can help get you there."

"Why should we trust you?" Lijun said.

"You already trusted me enough to come see me, then to bring me this news," Sunli said. "Tell me, what do you see when you look at me?"

Lijun gave him a crooked smile. "I see a man struggling to do his best. You have been touched by what is going on, but you haven't gone down the same path as my father. It's your eyes that are different. They have a glow to them, a pure golden light that I haven't seen in any other."

Sunli hadn't been expecting that in the least. "I am a priest of the Temple of Truth," he said after a short pause. "All I wanted was to be able to actually see the truth."

"That will get you killed, you know, here in the House of Cobalt. Seeing or speaking the truth," Lijun said.

"I know," Sunli said. The weight of his responsibility

settled more firmly on his shoulders. "It doesn't matter. We are here, now. And we must get you two out."

He didn't need to add anything more. Lijun knew how poor her chances of surviving were here in the House of Cobalt.

"I will contact my brother," Lijun said.

"And I will make arrangements," Sunli said. What, exactly, he wasn't certain. But surely his sight would take them far.

Hopefully far enough for the children to be guided to safety.

Sunli had no such hope for himself. He was already damned. It was just a matter of time.

Chapter Fifteen

HOUSE OF GOLD

UNNIR SIGHED as she listened to Vide. She was so tired, all the time. She hadn't been this tired when she'd been pregnant. Then again, the land had upheld her and sustained her through the worst of that.

This close to the border, while her sense of the land was strong, her ability to draw from it was not.

Unnir and Vide sat alone in her tent, surrounded by the armies of VeinHolders and warriors. Unnir understood the symbol she was providing to the troops. She stayed in the largest of the tents, the cloth tinted gold, the inside of it bright all day and all night. She'd caused the land under the tent to rise slightly so that she would be visible, a shining beacon of hope.

The cousins met in the front half of the tent, the section large enough to hold twenty warriors in full armor as well as large tables and chairs.

Vide would gather intelligence reports all day, amassing a large amount of information about how the fight was going. He was her official second in command, able to advise her where and how to spend her troops. She used her landsense as best she could, but Vide had a better sense of not only logistics but both strategy and tactics.

That he'd offered her all his skills and talents was telling. Instead of constantly fighting or belittling her, he was making her stronger and better.

Of course, that didn't stop his snide tongue from working overtime occasionally.

Vide had come to her concerned that Kinaki's troops had backed off early that afternoon.

"Why aren't we celebrating their pulling back?" Unnir had said. "They aren't winning. Maybe they're getting tired. Maybe they'll back off or go away."

She didn't really believe it was possible. Kinaki and that damned demon of his were determined to destroy her land. She shuddered every time she remembered how horribly corrupt the House of Cobalt's lands had become, how awful the earth there was.

They wanted to do the same in the House of Gold's lands.

They'd have to wait until she was dead before she'd allow them access, though.

"Oh, right," Vide said. "They're going to say it was all a misunderstanding and wonder why we all just can't be friends." The sarcasm was thick enough to cut with a knife.

Unnir shot a look at Vide, warning him. He glared back with equal heat.

He was dressed in casual clothes, a loose dark green shirt that went with his darker coloring, wide blue eyes that had never once looked innocent, a long face with harsh angles and thin lips made for sneering.

Only after Unnir made herself pause and really look at her cousin did she see his exhaustion. Fear haunted his eyes.

"I'm sorry," Unnir said softly. She reached out across the table and squeezed Vide's hand.

Her cousin startled so hard she was hard pressed not to giggle out loud. He blinked rapidly at her as if in shock.

They'd never been a family who touched or hugged. Yudur, her uncle, would have ridiculed any sort of connection between people, calling it weakness. Unnir kept a close physical relationship with her husband, as well as her little girl.

But that was always hidden away, out of sight of anyone and everyone.

Obviously, given Vide's shock, he needed a girlfriend. Or a boyfriend. She'd never been certain which way his interests lay.

"So what do you think that Kinaki's early withdrawal of his troops means?" Unnir said after she removed her hand and gave Vide time to compose himself.

"I," he paused, clearing his throat, "I think it means they're up to something."

"You don't have any proof, but you have a suspicion, right?" Unnir prompted.

"Yes," Vide said. He finally appeared to be back to normal. "So far, they've been stupidly persistent, focusing at this single point on our shared border."

Unnir nodded. It had surprised her how straightforward Kinaki was being. The place where the majority of the battles were occurring was in a direct line north from Jinyi, along the main trade route between the two houses.

"You've set guards along the rest of the border, though, correct?" Unnir said. She vaguely remembered talking about this days ago, when they'd started their initial planning. Putting guards with a strong sense of the land up and down the border, possibly strong enough that they'd be able to alert Unnir if something was going wrong.

She hadn't been thinking of those guards recently. She guiltily added it to her ever-lengthening list of things that she should do every morning and every evening, to reach out and see if the guards could report anything to her.

"I did," Vide said. "They haven't had anything to report before now."

"But you think they might soon?" Unnir guessed.

Vide nodded. "I don't have good intelligence when it comes to the warriors we're fighting. All I can tell you is what I've amalgamated since the battles have begun."

"Go on," Unnir said, encouraging her cousin.

He would have denied that he was a little obsessive about accumulating all those details. Unnir didn't tease him about it, wanting to encourage this vein in him.

She needed every advantage she could get.

"There appear to be three types of warriors who we're fighting," Vide said. "The large majority of them are idiots. They're strong, and they have some level of training. However, they appear to forget their training most of the time, and will fall for the most obvious of traps."

"All right," Unnir said, unsure of how this was related to the borders or to what Kinaki was planning.

"Then there are those who are strong, and who have training, but again, seem to forget it at least half of the time. The last type are the pure warriors, who have the best training, who see traps easily and avoid them. They are generally not as strong physically as the others, but they're a lot smarter," Vide concluded.

"And?" Unnir prompted, not seeing whatever it was that Vide wanted her to see.

"So, we know that Kinaki is corrupted by a demon," Vide said. "Which means that half the time, he thinks like a demon. Straightforward. Attack. Throw warriors at the problem, instead of working around it."

"Do you think the demon has finally gotten around to

asking the living part of Kinaki how to solve their problem?" Unnir said, trying to put the pieces together.

"Yes!" Vide said. He actually gave her a real smile, one not tempered with a sneer. "We're going to have a long discussion once this is over about the training and thinking that you need to instill in your VeinHolders. Fewer than half of them were able to follow my lead to the right conclusion."

"What will Kinaki do, now that he has his head?" Unnir asked.

"I think he'll spread his men out," Vide said. "As we'd originally thought. That he'll test the border in several places, while still trying to keep our focus here. Once he has successfully slipped more than one group in, they'll attack, and we'll be dealing with a force behind the border as well as the group on the other side."

"Tricky," Unnir said, nodding. "Smart," she added, bowing her head once to Vide. "But I assume that you have a plan to counter this potential?"

"You know me so well, LandHolder," Vide said with a smirk. "This is what I would advise you to do."

Unnir listened, alternately appalled and pleased with the plan.

It was audacious.

And neither Kinaki or whatever demon had corrupted him would ever expect it.

"Put it into place with my blessing," Unnir said.

"As you will," Vide said.

Before he could stand and scurry off, Unnir took his hand again. This time, he didn't start like a rabbit, but he did gulp. Worry filled his expression.

"Thank you," Unnir said. "I know we haven't been on the same side before this time. But I am very glad that we are now. Thank you."

Vide nodded and gave her a half grin, one that still

looked a little unsure. "I don't necessarily regret what I've done in the past," he said slowly. "However, I'm glad that we can both get over ourselves and work together. We need to survive this. All of us."

Unnir understood that Vide was talking of Emil. She'd barely seen her other cousin, but she'd heard the reports of how he was actually turning into a good leader of men.

"One last thing," Unnir warned.

Vide grew stiff and worried again.

"Take care of yourself," she said. She pushed some of the power of the land at him, willing into him to a bit more warmth and strength. "It won't do anyone any good if you work yourself to death."

Vide's expression held wonder. "I will, LandHolder."

After he'd left, Unnir wondered if perhaps the peace between her and her cousins might hold after the war.

It was one of the few remaining hopes she had left.

Chapter Sixteen

HOUSE OF PEARL

SHIMOKORO STOOD on the last of the foothills with Darikuto and Chuyoko, looking down onto the lands of the House of Crystal.

The summer had been kind to the land. Sunkissed green and gold meadows stretched out across the plains. Bees danced above the grass, making comforting buzzing sounds. Copses of dark woods could be seen in the distance, a cool respite from the brilliant sun. Left of them, to the north, stood the impassable mountains that marked the edges of these lands. Shimokoro knew that he couldn't actually feel any winds blowing from those snow-capped peaks, but it still seemed colder in that direction.

They were several days travel from the capital city of Nyati, which was east and a little north. Or it would take several days if they didn't have the LandHolder's touch.

The main trade road leading down out of the foothills was sturdy and well-maintained by Darikuto, wide enough for a large cart to travel along easily. Slight ruts showed where many wheels had passed over, ruts that Darikuto had smoothed out as they'd passed.

The army had traveled along the main trade routes from Yawatan, through the center of the lands of the House of Pearl, then cut over the hills. Surprisingly few merchants had been on the roads. Shimokoro would have thought that this would be the busiest time of year for them, carting goods from farms to markets.

Maybe the unrest from the House of Cobalt had spread and people were staying home. Or, more likely, they'd heard about the army approaching and had decided to stay out of the way.

The trade road seemed to disappear just past the border of the lands. Shimokoro assumed that they were at an odd angle and that the road continued all the way to Nyati, where Darikuto would be welcomed as a savior.

The group would make their way across the border later that morning, then continue traveling for a day, maybe two. Darikuto wanted to stop well short of the capital to do his spells, to bring the land to his rule. Not quite in the center of the land, but close to it.

Shimokoro felt a thrill go through him when Darikuto gave the signal for the army to start forward again. He was about to be a part of history. Oh, the songs they'd sing about today!

Joyously, he strode forward, certain of his place in history as one of the main implementers of the glorious Plan.

DOUBT CREPT over Shimokoro when he realized that there was no road on the far side of the border. The path just... vanished. It was as if there had never been a road. He couldn't even see a shadow of where it might have been.

Instead, fields of wild grasses grew where the road ended. Not short grass either, but grasses tall enough to have been growing all summer long. The edge between the two wasn't as abrupt as he'd thought it might be: some of those same grasses had starting to creep along the road, making their way into the lands of the House of Pearl.

Darikuto had frowned when he'd seen them, flattening them immediately and making the road solid gravel again.

But the sprouts were stubborn. Shimokoro saw a few poking back up through the road after the LandHolder had passed.

Were the untamed, unsettled lands of the House of Crystal trying to infect the lands of the House of Pearl? That was what it felt like. Given Darikuto's serious expression, Shimokoro wondered how far the border between the two lands had shifted without him noticing it.

No matter. As soon as Darikuto took possession of this wild land, the border would be irrelevant.

While they'd been in the House of Pearl's lands, Darikuto had easily lifted the entire army along, so that every step the people took was the equivalent of dozens of normal steps. Thus, instead of taking weeks or months to cross from Yawatan to the border, it had taken them two days.

Their progress abruptly slowed when they reached the border. Shimokoro suddenly felt the full weight of the pack he carried. He started sweating, feeling the heat of the sun pounding down on his bare head. It took more effort to pass through knee-high grass than on a flat road. The humming of insects took on a high-pitched, annoying whine. At least the sun-baked grasses smelled sweet.

The heads of the other temples traveled beside him, the four of them dressed casually, each carrying their own rucksack as well as more supplies in trunks being hauled behind the group. They all appeared to feel the same way, grimacing at each other as their pace slowed.

Shimokoro reached out with his landsense. The land here

felt aloof. He'd experienced that before, when he'd traveled the previous year with Darikuto to the House of Gold's lands, when they'd gone for the annual summer meeting of the LandHolders.

It lightened his heart that the land felt so normal here. He'd had a moment of worry that though it had been less than a week, that the land would have grown wild and been difficult to bring under Darikuto's rule.

Still, looking around, he sensed that something was wrong here. He just couldn't put his finger on it, though.

The sun beat down on them as they crossed the unending sea of grass. Shimokoro felt overly warm in his trousers, boots, and long-sleeved shirt. He hadn't bothered wearing formal robes, though those were packed in his travel trunk. He wished for a fisherman's hat—wide brimmed and made of woven reeds—the kind that would shelter his head and shade his eyes.

Shimokoro tried to call up a small breeze to cool himself off.

None came to his calling.

Strange. He'd been able to do simple things like that when they'd visited the House of Gold, or even the House of Cobalt's lands, as corrupt as those had been.

He tried it again, but there was no breeze to be had.

Very odd. Of course, he had no ability at augury these days, so he couldn't foresee if this was a large problem or just a small one.

After they'd been walking for at least a couple of hours, Shimokoro finally saw a dark forest on the horizon. He was looking forward to getting out of the sun, into the cool shade of the trees. He walked a little more briskly, only noticing in passing that the grass had started growing taller. It passed his knees and was now mid-thigh. It was a little more difficult to pass through.

Then the edges of the leaves grew sharp.

It was the same grass they'd been walking through before. Shimokoro would swear that it hadn't changed.

But now, when he swung his hands, brushing carefree through the grass, he ended up with tiny cuts, faint white marks against his dark skin.

Darikuto appeared to notice at the same time and signaled a halt. The messenger beside him raised a conch shell and blew, the trilling notes carried on the still air, then the notes were picked up and repeated by other messengers down the line.

"This land—it resents us," Darikuto said after a few moments.

Shimokoro didn't have as strong of a sense of the land as the LandHolder. However, he believed it. The land had swallowed the road.

Suddenly, Shimokoro realized what had been bothering him before.

There should have been farms, possibly a village or two, close to the border, to ensure that the House of Pearl didn't try to push across and gain more land. In the bad old days, before the peace, there might have been warriors, maybe even a CrystalHolder, waiting at the border as well.

Where were the farmers? Where were the fields? It was just grass and the dark spot of the trees.

Despite the heat, Shimokoro felt a chill race down his spine.

Only now did he feel the resentment that the land bore toward them.

It wasn't the corruption of the House of Cobalt's lands. No, as Darikuto had said, walking across those lands felt more like stepping on ash instead of solid dirt.

Here, the land seethed with an underlying anger. Shimokoro suddenly felt exposed standing there in the middle of the field, where everything could see him and he had no cover.

Darikuto talked quietly with Chuyoko for a few moments, then stood waiting as she turned and started spreading the news.

"This land has killed," Darikuto told Shimokoro and the other priests standing in a group to the side.

The others gasped. Shimokoro found a hard, dry lump in his throat that he swallowed past.

"Stay together," Darikuto warned. "We will set guard tonight, to make sure that none get taken. And don't go into the woods. The trees there are...wild."

Shimokoro nodded grimly. Seemed the land had grown far more aware since the passing of Ibitsima.

Was this to be Darikuto's grand failing? As with the House of Cobalt, had his plans been too successful?

Shimokoro shook his head, pushing aside his doubt.

No, Darikuto was going to succeed. He would wear the mantle of both lands on his shoulders. They would persevere.

Their place in history was assured.

Or so he told himself despite the chills that continued to race up and down his spine.

Chapter Seventeen
HOUSE OF CRYSTAL

MENHAPTU SLAPPED his hand down on his desk. The loud sound echoed off the marble walls of his office like a crack of thunder.

Baka, the head of the CrystalHolders, sat on the other side of Menhaptu's desk looking as stunned as if Menhaptu had just slapped him.

"That isn't good enough," Menhaptu repeated. "There is a foreign army approaching our border. They might already be here! And yet, you continue to insist that we do nothing. Why?"

Baka glared at him, as if Menhaptu were still just an apprentice or acolyte. The head of the CrystalHolders was short for someone from the House of Gold, almost as short as someone from the House of Cobalt. His skin was leathery and reddened from being outside so much. He had a long face with bulging eyes, that Menhaptu unkindly likened to that of a goat. To be fair, he also had bulging muscles that he showed off that morning, wearing a sleeveless gray tunic, as well as pants that were tight enough to display his thighs as well.

"We have no LandHolder," Baka repeated, speaking slowly as if Menhaptu were particularly young or dense. Or perhaps both. "Darikuto, even if he never takes hold of the mantel of the House of Crystal, is still infinitely stronger. He can support his warriors. Heal them. Trying to fight him, or them, is just throwing away the lives of good warriors."

"So we should just roll over and let him take us?" Menhaptu said with as much scorn as he could muster. "Dishonor the memory of Ibitsima? Forget what it was like to be able to stand on our own, free of a foreign LandHolder?"

Baka didn't reply, so Menhaptu pressed on. "Or are your warriors so weak, their training so poor, that they couldn't do any good? That they'd be slaughtered immediately, like you say?"

"My warriors are the best, the fiercest, in all the lands," Baka barked back in reply. "I just don't want to lead them to an unnecessary battle."

"The land needs time to choose," Menhaptu said smoothly. "You and your warriors need to buy it that time. I don't expect you to be able to turn back a foreign army, not without a LandHolder. You just need to delay them."

"The land isn't going to choose," Baka said. "Or if it has, the new Holder has refused."

Menhaptu pressed his lips together instead of instantly denying the accusation. He'd heard the same arguments before, from the other heads of the temples. The land *must* have already chosen another LandHolder. And they'd refused, for whatever reason.

"The land *will* choose. We just have to give it time," Menhaptu insisted after a moment.

"What?" Baka asked. "Have you *seen* it?"

Menhaptu opened his mouth then shut it again. Augury

was not merely impossible, but dangerous in an untamed land. Who knew what would happen if he tried?

"I thought not," Baka sneered. "It's just as useless for you to try peering into the smoke and crystals as it is for us to go fight."

"I will make you a bargain," Menhaptu said. He felt the words pouring out of him, as if they came, unprompted, from somewhere else. "I will direct my acolytes back to seeking the future. And I will try myself as well. But only if you will send warriors out to at least harass the approaching army."

Baka narrowed his eyes and stared at Menhaptu, as if trying to see the truth, or maybe the source, those brave words had sprung from.

"Very well," Baka said slowly. "If you are willing to risk your followers, as well as your own hide, for what is likely to be a dangerous and fruitless task, who am I to do any less? We will leave in the morning."

Baka nodded sharply at Menhaptu, then stood and strode out of the door.

Menhaptu sat back in his chair, feeling all the energy and life drain out of him. Whatever had been propping him up, and prompting him, had vanished.

Had it been the land wanting him to try new forms of divination? Just as much as he'd wanted Baka and the warriors to do something?

Menhaptu had checked the heart of the Chamber of Crystals every day. The corruption at the heart of it continued to grow, albeit slowly. Was there some connection between that darkness and his rash words?

He had no idea.

Regardless of the source, it felt right for him to do something. Anything was better than merely sitting in Nyati, waiting.

Even if it was dangerous, and meant the death of some of the acolytes who would be taken by explosive magic.

Standing, Menhaptu felt the world grow dark around the edges of his vision. He swayed, then pushed himself upright.

He must be more tired than he thought. Or more drained by whatever had possessed him.

However, he would do this. He would prove to Baka and the others that he was a good fit for the Head of the Temple of Truth.

And he would survive this, at least long enough to get his revenge on the other priests who were still hiding.

Chapter Eighteen
HOUSE OF COBALT

KINAKI FELT the demon Wanho shift, the coils entrapping his body sliding a little. He concentrated on what he was saying, not allowing a break in his speech to the CollierHolders in front of him. It was important that he convey his plan carefully and fully, and that the warriors see him as a strong LandHolder, not one divided.

They all stood in his private tent, erected to the side of the battlefield. The canvas had been colored a marvelous, soothing blue. Instead of ropes, living vines dotted with hanging white bell-like flowers held up the poles. The ground was good solid dirt—none of those fancy carpets or floor coverings for him. Humid air filled the tent, as there were at least twenty warriors in here with Kinaki. Though he'd brought a throne, he stood for now on the platform at one end of the tent, exhorting his warriors.

Wanho shifted slightly again. It had taken time and practice for Kinaki to be able to maintain his focus when Wanho moved. At first, he'd thought the shifting deliberate, that the demon was trying to get his attention.

But Kinaki had learned much of the nature of demons.

They were straight forward. When Wanho wanted something, he'd whisper in Kinaki's ear. The shifting around was actually a nervous habit of Wanho's, like a man sitting in a chair and occasionally fidgeting.

The demon was understandably nervous. He did but he didn't fully comprehend this new strategy that Kinaki had proposed, why slipping behind the enemy's lines would work, why it wouldn't end in immediate slaughter.

Kinaki knew that he would lose warriors through such a bold move. But it would also distract Unnir, at a time when she was most vulnerable.

At least that was what he kept saying, kept telling himself and others. He never thought about the truth, not even when he was doing exercises with other warriors in the mornings.

How this would weaken his army at the greatest point of contact, and how this might allow for Unnir to actually push him back.

Kinaki understood that he was a divided man. Part of his soul longed for the lands of the House of Gold, to taste them, to hold them, to rule over them.

There was a small, very small part, though, that was repulsed by what it saw, what Kinaki had become, all in the desire to live and rule just a bit longer.

He couldn't see the endgame. Or rather, he couldn't admit it to himself, that all this only ended with his head on a pike. He also knew that he would continue to fight until the bitter end.

As he finished laying out his plan, a messenger came in. The messenger stood just inside the entrance of the tent. Obviously she had important news—just not important enough to interrupt the current work being done.

Soon enough, Kinaki dismissed the CollierHolders and signaled the messenger to come forward. He sat down on this throne now, surprisingly tired.

Generally, Wanho kept up Kinaki's strength. But Kinaki had been talking to CollierHolders, not the WarHolders. The group had been mostly composed of the living, not demons. They needed to maintain a level of subtlety that was foreign to most demons.

Maybe being isolated from others of his kind had weakened Wanho?

Kinaki would have to remember to think about that the next morning, when he did his morning exercises with the other warriors.

"Come, come," he said, gesturing for the messenger to approach.

"Thank you, LandHolder," the woman said in a surprisingly deep voice. She was short, even for someone from the House of Cobalt, perhaps merely four and a half feet tall. It would be easy to mistake her for a child or teenager.

One look at her face would disabuse the viewer of that notion, however. It was lined with age and grief. Her reddish skin looked muddy and worn. Black eyes filled with pain stared out above hollowed cheeks. She wore a simple robe cut from rough, gray cloth and belted around her waist, with plain sandals.

"What news do you have?" Kinaki asked as he poured himself a cup of water.

"There is no easy way to say this, my lord," the woman said gravely. She paused, taking a deep breath, before she continued. "Chaotu, your son, is dead. And your daughter, Lijun, is missing."

Kinaki gasped. Though he'd sent guards out after Chaotu, he'd assumed that the boy would somehow escape. He'd been the smartest of them all. And Lijun, well, he'd bet that the priests had something to do with her hiding. She'd always been far too religious for his tastes, trusting to the gods and augury instead of hard work.

Tears sprang to Kinaki's eyes. He didn't remember the last time he'd wept. It certainly hadn't been when his wife had told him that she'd no longer return to his private chambers, that his tastes had gotten too extreme for her.

That was of little matter, though he did remember vaguely loving her at one point.

Before.

Rage infused Kinaki. He tilted his head back and gave a loud howl. Winds sprang up and the sides of the tent bowed and flexed as they rushed this way and that, unsure where to settle.

Finally, Kinaki got hold of himself. Wanho remained silent through all of his rage and sorrow.

As still as a statue as well.

"What happened to Chaotu?" Kinaki said, the words grinding out like rough gravel. "How did he die?"

"Rogues—we're assuming from the House of Gold—had the audacity to dress as *your* guards," the messenger said. Her affront was obvious. "They attacked the Hold that you'd sent your son to for his safety. True guards, guards who were loyal to you, learned of the attack, but didn't arrive in time to stop the marauders. No one was left alive. The assassins were killed immediately, as soon as they were discovered."

Another wave of grief washed over Kinaki. Had there actually been attackers from the House of Gold? He wouldn't have put it past Yudur, the previous LandHolder. Not Unnir, however. She was too weak too stomach such action.

No, it was likely the "true" guards killed their compatriots and burned the place down afterward, to hide the conspiracy.

"And Lijun?" Kinaki said after a moment, when he felt as though he could breathe again.

"Unsure," the messenger said. "She'd been staying at a different Hold. However, when the guards went to find her, they were told that she'd vanished the night before. No one knew where she was. None at the Hold appeared to have aided her."

Kinaki nodded grimly. He knew that the Holder and all of her kin had probably all been tortured for what little information they had.

"Thank you," Kinaki said slowly. "I will see to it that the House of Gold pays dearly for the grief they've caused," Kinaki added as he stood.

The messenger bowed and left.

Kinaki sat, feeling his grief confound him again. Such a waste! He hadn't wanted to order the execution of his children. He was truly grieved at their demise. He'd tried to get Chaotu to follow him, to bend in his direction, but his son had arrogantly said he'd rather die first.

So be it.

But it was all for the best. Now, none opposed him.

"We must tell the warriors of the atrocities that the House of Gold has enacted on us," Kinaki said, speaking out loud to Wanho.

Yes. Let's use this, came the whispered reply.

"Now you see why sneaking into their lands is a good action," Kinaki continued. "It's what the living do."

Again, Kinaki felt the demon's body shifting, moving itself slightly to a more comfortable position. But then Wanho settled, the weight imagined and comforting.

Kinaki would never escape the demon's clutches alive.

But in his secret heart of hearts, he also hoped that when it came time, he would take the demon with him when he died, the pair of them descending to the underworld, there to battle each other evermore.

Chapter Nineteen

HOUSE OF GOLD

TORJA DREAMED OF WIND.

She was still in her tent on the edge of the battlefield. She knew in that perfect logic of dreams that she was the only one who could see the curious breeze as it blew from one end of the tent to the other, stirring the grass and dirt, then swirling up like a geyser. It passed over the sheets of her cot like an absent-minded hand seeking the comfort of worn things. Smells of pines, long baked in the summer sun, traveled with it.

However, it was a very polite wind, at least as far as Torja could judge. It didn't bellow out the sides of her tent, but stayed just inside, even as she could tell it grew more impatient.

Torja's dream self finally rose to do the wind's bidding. It swirled around her ankles like a friendly litter of puppies finally being let out into the yard. She had to be careful or it would trip her.

Outside, the world had changed. Hers was the only tent that remained in this great empty bowl of land. There were no signs of the recent conflict—the land had healed itself and tall summer grass filled the area. It was still night, and the moon silvered the area, showing her soft light. The smell of mint mingled with bitter daisies.

Torja's outfit changed from her nightgown to more formal robes.

But the robes were different than what she normally wore.

All robes worn by those from the House of Gold had long sleeves and oversized cuffs. Torja had always despaired of wearing them, as she just didn't have the grace to pull them off. She was forever dragging the cuffs against something, knocking things over with them. They just weren't practical.

She was still shocked to find her arms free and bare. The rest of the robe covered her completely, made out of green cotton and belted at the waist. Beautiful embroidered plaques went down the front of the robe, lining the hem as well as the collar. It was a rolling pattern of spears of wheat. The gold thread sparkled as she walked, filling her heart with joy.

They reminded her of the fletche she used in her foretelling. However, the pieces of braided wheat were stiff while the embroidered wheat was so fluid, like a tumbling river.

The wind herded Torja along, still polite, nudging her away from the center of the hollowed-out meadow in front of her and off to the side.

It took her a moment to realize that she was supposed to go to the east.

Of course, that was the true place of power.

The grass grew spiky under her bare feet as she skirted a boulder. She found herself stepping sharply, not walking, more like skipping. The less amount of time that her skin made contact with the grass, the less it pricked her.

Soon, she was skipping and hopping along. She did, but didn't realize she was in a dream. She didn't feel embarrassed by her actions—no one could see her.

No one living, that was. It wasn't until she leaped to the top of the rim of the bowl that she realized that she did have an audience.

On the far side of the hill a sea of ghosts waited for her. Torja had never seen so many gathered in a single place before. Cold emanated off them, like winds blowing off snowy peaks. They floated like clouds, glowing brightly. The moonlight seemed harsher now, and a long, distinct shadow now flowed out behind Torja.

She found she still couldn't stand still. She had to shuffle her feet, or step lively in place.

Finally came the whispered word, carried by all the ghostly throats before her.

Dance.

Torja stopped moving in surprise. She didn't dance. Not really. She'd been taught simple country dances when she was a child. But she'd never bothered learning the fancy footwork and gestures the court dances had.

However, none of those seemed appropriate. She had no partner, there was no music to listen to. Plus, given how she was forced to move from one foot to the other so quickly, even a quick jig didn't feel right.

Torja tried to imagine an appropriate ghostly tune for her circumstances, something quick. Maybe even lively.

Not even her imagination was good enough for that, though.

The friendly wind came back to see her, the one that had visited her in her tent. She didn't know how she knew this, as it appeared that most winds looked alike, but she did. Her wind wasn't merely white and blustery—it had a pale gold tint to it every now and again, a shimmer that sparked in the pale moonlight.

The wind whirled around her. She turned in place, as if trying to chase it. Though she felt more like a clumsy puppy trying to catch her own tail.

The image made her smile, and she twirled more, faster, harder. The wind matched her speed, lending her its strength as she grew tired. She felt her thoughts start to float up above her head as her body spun like a top.

Up here, she could see far off in the distance, as if the miles no longer mattered.

A dark cloud blossomed on the horizon to the east.

Curious, Torja directed her thoughts that way, trying to see what was there.

Two pillars of light were crossing into the land, chased by a vile, corrupted cloud.

Torja knew that the pillars represented people, people who she needed to meet, people who were important to the House of Gold lands. Just as she needed to repulse the thing that chased after them.

She felt her breath catch when she realized the significance of what she was seeing.

It was a vision, granted to her by the power of the ghosts spread out before her, carried on the winds and her own effort.

It was a new way to cast an augury, to dance and spin, invoking the winds to bring her visions.

Torja found herself drifting back to her body before she could see more. She wanted to yell, to curse.

She'd finally gotten her sight back, only to be denied it again. It hadn't been long enough! She wanted, *needed* to see more.

When she looked down on her body she saw why she couldn't continue. She was starting to slow down. She didn't have the strength to dance forever. She'd recovered from her previous ordeal, when she'd used the fire to learn the true nature of the House of Cobalt, but dancing in this manner was another matter entirely.

She slowly floated down into her body, like a down feather drifting back and forth. Her exhaustion slammed into her as if it were her real body, and not just a dream.

Except that when she fully regained consciousness, she found that she was no longer in her tent, but standing on a hill near the camp. Guards stood all around her, a few feet away. As did Ragna, Torja's accomplice and acolyte.

Torja slumped over, her legs shaking and weak. Ragna rushed over to support her. Torja gratefully allowed the other woman to take some of her weight.

Torja tried to ask what happened, but her throat was so dry all that came out was a croak.

"After you started sleepwalking, and the guards couldn't wake you, they came to get me," Ragna explained anyway. "We all followed you up here. Then you started to spin. Slowly at first. Then faster and faster. I could *see* the magic flowing off you, that rose higher and higher as you danced."

"Augury," Torja finally managed to push out her parched throat.

Ragna merely nodded and didn't ask what Torja had seen, though Torja knew that the other woman really wanted to know.

"So, the next time you invent a new form of augury, you think you could give me some warning first?" Ragna teased after a few moments.

Torja wearily nodded.

She needed food and drink.

As well as the fastest guards Unnir could supply.

Her destiny lay to the east. And she was eager to meet it.

Chapter Twenty

HOUSE OF PEARL

CHUYOKO TRIED to contain her growl as she stalked away from the most recent incident, heading back to her own small tent for the rest of the evening.

Fools. All of them.

This land was *wild*. It didn't know the taming influence of a LandHolder's touch. It had overgrown the hold—and possibly an entire village—that had been located at the border, killing all those living there.

Magic came from one's sense of the land. Everyone had the ability to cast simple magic, such as to light a fire, set rocks to heat or stay cool, or to clean and repair clothes. Those with more landsense generally had stronger magic. They could build houses, bring up water for crops, and keep away the bugs that plagued cattle and people alike.

Warriors generally didn't have a lot of landsense. They focused their abilities inward, to train their bodies for combat. None matched Chuyoko in fierce determination and skill, though there were a few who'd started training with her during this journey, rising with her in the early mornings.

They wouldn't continue once they made it back to the cushy city. None were as dedicated as she.

Still, the fools should have known better than to try drawing up a large amount of magic here.

At least they hadn't killed themselves when the stones they'd heated grew too hot and exploded. Or perhaps that would have been a good thing, as that would mean fewer idiots she'd have to deal with.

She'd quickly spread word through the camped army to not use magic. She was too late, of course. Other reports from the widespread tents came back of accidents, from candles melting to ground buckling when someone had tried smoothing it out.

The priests had stopped trying to cast auguries, to peer into pools and see the future, a while ago.

Now it was time for the warriors to fall back on their physical training. There would be no magical aid for any of their attacks, nothing to guide their hand when they struck. The land here would just as soon drain them as support them, so they wouldn't be able to heal themselves either.

But who was going to attack them? There hadn't been a garrison at the border. No guards to turn them back.

No, just an angry, unsettled land that hated them, and was going to do its best to destroy them.

How did she battle the land itself?

CHUYOKO DIDN'T BOTHER HIDING her stony expression as she walked out of the meeting with Darikuto, Shimokoro, and the various PearlHolders. However, she was in control of herself enough that she didn't storm out of the tent, but walked briskly back toward her people. The sun had already cleared the horizon, and it was going to be another hot day on the sunbaked planes.

The previous night had been bad. Vines had crept in, vines that the sentries hadn't been able to see because they couldn't cast any magical light.

Vines that had pushed themselves up onto the cots of sleeping warriors, then had strangled them in their sleep.

Not every warrior, no. But every second or third one. The selection seemed random to Chuyoko.

Or perhaps the land had chosen to be so random in order to guarantee maximum terror.

They'd been reduced by a third overnight.

However, those *fools* just wanted to continue as if nothing had happened.

Chuyoko walked over to Orinmegu, her second in command. He was a dour youngster, who appeared much older than he actually was. His scowl was as constant as his dark-colored skin. His head rose up a good six inches over hers. Others might find his size and mien threatening. Chuyoko had come to rely on him like a good strong pike, used to keep others at bay.

"What did they say?" Orinmegu growled.

Chuyoko was grateful that he sounded angry. He'd follow her lead in everything.

"Nothing." Chuyoko spit out the word. "We aren't to change anything. Just proceed like normal."

Orinmegu grunted and nodded, obviously waiting to hear what they were going to do instead.

However, Chuyoko didn't know what they needed to do. How could she fight the land? They couldn't see the threats in the dark, couldn't call up magic to light their way.

The silence drew on, Chuyoko going through and discarding plan after plan.

Finally, Orinmegu cleared his throat. "May I make a suggestion?"

"Yes," Chuyoko said. Maybe the young man had a better idea.

"Keep a minimal guard on the perimeter of the camp. Reconfigure the tents to hold twenty or more. Keep watch inside, instead," Orinmegu said.

"I suggested that," Chuyoko said, letting all the bitterness she was feeling come out. "I was out-voted. By Darikuto."

Orinmegu took a deep breath, then let it out, nodding. In normal times, that would be the end of the argument. One didn't disagree with the LandHolder.

"We are going to do it anyway," Chuyoko added, dropping her voice down.

Orinmegu raised his eyebrows, surprised.

"If we can't reconfigure the tents, as no one has the magic to do it without consequences," Chuyoko continued, "we might, instead, just have guards patrolling in and out of them."

It had shocked her that Darikuto had admitted that he didn't trust his own magic at that point. The land was too unforgiving. He could do some things, more than the average warrior. But he wanted to save all his strength for the spells he'd need to cast to draw the land to him.

"I'll make sure they get set back up tonight in a tight pattern," Orinmegu volunteered.

"Thank you," Chuyoko said. She knew that she could rely on him.

It didn't bear thinking that she might, *might*, not be able to rely fully on her LandHolder anymore.

CHUYOKO LISTENED to reports first thing the next morning. The false dawn cast a chilled light between the tents. She sat on the ground in her tent, sipping hot green tea as one after another messenger came in to inform her what had occurred during the evening.

Other PearlHolders had a single report to listen to. Chuyoko had tried that, but found too much was summarized, and she didn't get enough of the details that she needed. Therefore, she always had more than one person reporting on the same events, so that she could distill the truth out of them after combining them.

All the warriors were spooked. It was one thing to face an enemy. Even a demon. It was something completely different to be uncertain about the ground you walked on.

Still, there was something *off* in the warrior's report she was listening to.

"Wait, go over that part again," she directed.

"The bushes on the edges of the camp. They moved last night," the warrior stated. "And one of them attacked Juinkoi," he insisted.

"That isn't possible," Chuyoko said. She shook her head. "No, a large bush or a tree moves slowly. Too slowly to attack." She put her tea to the side and stood. "Show me where this attack occurred."

She followed the warrior out into the brisk dawn. Too soon, the sun would drive away all the coolness, punishing them with heat. She missed the cool breezes from the ocean, the shade of trees.

They wound their way through the closely pitched tents out to the perimeter. A grass filled plane stretched to the horizon. A few copses of trees were off in the distance. Had they moved overnight? She couldn't be certain.

Scraggly bushes stuck out above the grass. She didn't

recognize the plant. Something both viney and leafy, that grew in a rough ball shape.

She reached out and tugged at the one closest. It resisted, staying exactly where it was.

The second one moved easily, rolling away from where it had been resting.

Chuyoko knelt down to where the plant had been sitting.

It had been hiding a footprint in the baked soil.

She stood up and looked out. She couldn't see anything, of course. Just the grass waving slightly in the breeze that came up every dawn. It sent a quiet shiver down her spine.

The warrior standing beside her flinched when she turned to face him.

Good.

"This was not an attack from the land. This was from another warrior, hiding behind a bush, using it as camouflage." Chuyoko felt a fierce grin take over her face. "We have company."

It was one thing to try to fight the land, to overcome something so amorphous.

It was quite another, though, to finally have a real enemy to face.

Chapter Twenty-One
HOUSE OF CRYSTAL

Yimifut stubbornly sat on what he called the river rock, watching the water pass underneath him. It was his favorite place in all of the Hold. Dappled sunlight shone through the green leaves towering above him. The water sparkled and splashed, a steady wash of quiet sound. A nest with baby birds chirped loudly in a tree beside him, constantly hungry.

It was the one place where Yimifut could ignore everything else going on in the Hold right now: how uncertain his mother Sitre was and how her hold on the land was slipping steadily as the days passed and no LandHolder stepped forward; the anger of the land at being used and shaped by people and not allowed to grow as wild as it yearned to be; and the Land, that cloak of power, that still lurked, following him and demanding that he dedicate his life to it.

Yimifut had always known that the Land would seek him out one day. He'd had a gift for foretelling that the priests didn't understand. He knew the consequences of accepting the burden of the Land.

So many people would die.

So many people had already died, though, as the land asserted itself. Farms and villages swallowed by rapacious fields, finding themselves buried alive as the grasses spread. Or when the forests moved away from their usual setting, the trees slowly stepping beyond the spaces that had been left for them, not just demanding more, but stealing it away from where people had been.

However, Yimifut couldn't take on the mantel of the land. Not yet.

Not until he understood *why*.

Why would the Land seek him? He was just a boy. Barely fifteen, despite the fact that everyone said he had an old soul —whatever that meant. He was a Holder's son, and his magic was stronger than most.

But surely there were others who were even stronger. So it wasn't strength that made the Land seek him out.

His parents, as well as his siblings, knew just how stubborn Yimifut could be. His father still told the story of when Yimifut was three years old, and they were trying to get him to go to bed. They took his toys away. Then the rest of the clothes. They finally realized that he would end up naked in an empty room before he would give in.

When they relented and said that he could go to bed whenever he wanted, he merely nodded at them, then toddled off to bed on his own.

So while Yimifut was more stubborn than most, there had to be some other attribute that the land sought.

His mother Sitre would have welcomed the Land if it had come to her. She was as rough and as rugged as the headlands, where the hills first bore the brunt of the winter winds. Her face was ruddy from being out in storms. She wasn't as tall as most, but was thicker, more solid, as if her bones were heavier. No mere wind was about to blow her over.

Yimifut wouldn't give the land to her, though such thoughts made him feel as if he were betraying his family. However, Sitre would just grow rough given more power. The land with its new Holder would remain aloof. People's lives would be more difficult, not easier, with that sort of LandHolder.

No, Yimifut would have to decide, and soon, whether to take the land or to allow a foreign power to hold it. He'd always known that this crisis would arrive one day. He could see a few of the consequences of his choices. Then, his visions disappeared.

No one, not even the gods themselves, knew what happened after that.

That also held him in place. He'd grown used to his knowledge of what came next.

He'd be operating blindly, just as the priests of the Temple of Truth were these days.

Still, Yimifut hesitated. If he didn't understand *why* the land had chosen him, then he couldn't focus on that ability, couldn't get any better at it. And while he'd accept no longer knowing the future, he needed some sort of guidance.

He hoped that Akalina and her ghosts would be able to tell him, that they'd show him a dark reflection of himself.

When he'd first met Akalina a few years before, he didn't understand what the whiteness of the cloak, or aura surrounding her, meant. It hadn't been until this year that he'd been able to start connecting the colors of the auras with patterns of behavior.

No one else could see the auras, he knew that. He also knew that ability would disappear once he accepted the mantle of the land. It wasn't something that the land needed. He'd be connected to people in a different manner, instead.

He heard someone climbing the rocks behind him,

climbing up from the walk beside the river, and up to the point itself.

Though he'd known this day was coming, he still sighed. He wished for a few more days before the terrible choice was upon him, a few more days of freedom.

He turned though, and nodded at Akalina. "Welcome," he made himself say, though the word tasted bitter.

She looked older than he remembered. Her face looked pinched and drawn, as if she were in pain. Wisps of black hair escaped the braid down her back, framing her face with a dark halo that extended out into the white aura that only he could see.

He found it interesting that her aura had gotten stronger, while most, since Ibitsima had died, had gotten smaller and weaker. He didn't know why, though. So many ghosts had disappeared in the last couple of years. Were they flocking to her for protection?

"Thank you," Akalina said. She didn't ask, but came to sit down beside him.

They spent a few blissful moments like that, looking out on the water, listening to the birds, feeling the soft breezes.

Finally, Akalina said, "You know why I'm here, I'm guessing."

Yimifut nodded. "I do." He felt grateful that Akalina remembered his abilities to tell the future, and believed him. No one else did.

"Why won't you take the mantle of the land?" Akalina said after another short pause. "Will something horrible happen if you do?"

Yimifut shrugged. "Yes. And no. Terrible things will happen if I don't."

"Then what's stopping you?" Akalina demanded. "I don't understand."

"The land is cold," Yimifut said after a few moments.

Akalina nodded and gave a brief shiver. She knew. She was the only one who did, whom he could share that knowledge with.

"The land changes the person who becomes the LandHolder," he continued.

She nodded cautiously. It was something that, while known, was never spoken of. If anything was ever said, it was always couched in the most complimentary of terms, how becoming a LandHolder made the person better, if anything was said at all.

"The land will change me," Yimifut said, trying to put everything he felt into words. "But how will I know what to hold onto, or to embrace, if I don't understand why the land has chosen me in the first place?"

Akalina thought for a moment. "I've always thought that the land initially chose me because of my connection to the ghosts." She paused, then continued. "I have a strong landsense, but a stronger ghost-sense, as it were. The ghosts aren't just connected to our past, but also to our future. Without the ghosts, there is no augury. No foretelling. Our past makes our future possible."

Yimifut merely nodded, though he hadn't thought of that before.

"You must have some sort of connection to the future, if not through the ghosts, then through something else, that the land senses and needs," Akalina finished.

"The land didn't settle with you because the ghosts made you barren," Yimifut said after a few moments.

Akalina flinched, then she firmly nodded. "I know."

"So you think that there's something connecting me to the future? Something I can't see? That is why the land chose me?" Yimifut asked, trying to clarify.

"Yes," Akalina said. Then she shook her head. "No. You've always been able to see the future. But people who have great augury ability aren't necessarily chosen to become a LandHolder."

Yimifut nodded. "And at some point, after I make my final decision, either I lose the ability, or the future is so unclear it can't be predicted."

"Could it be that you'll have a great heir? Someone that the land needs in the future?" Akalina guessed.

"That's too far out," Yimifut said firmly. "And it's too unpredictable. Augury isn't always accurate. No, it has to be something to do with me. And until I figure it out, I will not take on the mantle of the land."

Akalina looked as if she wanted to say more. However, she looked at him, pressed her lips together, then shook her head. "You will need to decide soon. Or the land will be lost."

"I know," Yimifut said. And though there were few things that scared him, this choice was one of them.

That he'd either make the wrong choice, or he'd make it too late.

It was a heavy burden for someone so young to bear, even if he'd been born with an old soul.

Chapter Twenty-Two

HOUSE OF COBALT

SUNLI DRAGGED BEHIND THE OTHERS, as usual. He found it difficult to keep up with the brisk pace set by Chaotu and Lijun, to say nothing of the two warriors who accompanied them, both of whom were young and fit.

Whereas Sunli was older, out of shape (and frequently out of breath) and he was fighting with his demon Belam constantly.

Belam had been silent for much of his occupancy of Sunli. However, since they'd left Jinyi, the demon had become demanding. He hadn't wanted to leave the city, didn't see the point. He'd granted Sunli the ability to see into a person's soul, as well as to see the full corruption of the land.

Out here in the middle of nowhere, there were no people to view and judge. The land, while corrupted, wasn't anything new. There was nothing to shock Sunli with. And it had taken Sunli a while to appreciate that Belam enjoyed shocking his host.

Therefore, Belam made it difficult for Sunli to continue, held him back.

Chaotu and the guards would have left Sunli behind days ago. Only Lijun's insistence had kept the party together.

They were passing through foothills now. Sunli cursed every hill he saw. Maybe his old bones could have made it across a flat plane. But the hills mocked him and had him scrambling like a goat.

His shirt was sweat-stained, his pants, muddy. Even the hat he wore to protect himself from the merciless sun was battered and torn. He'd have to burn it all when he got back to the city. At least he had some decent boots. Not that he could ever wear them inside a temple. Ugh.

He carried his own backpack, knowing it was the least he could do. It was built out of a sturdy wooden frame with canvas stretched over it.

In his daydreams he'd burn his pack first, feeding the wood lovingly into the fire.

There weren't details that he could distract himself with either. It was the same monotonous rising and falling of hills and land. Even the corpse flowers and spike weeds no longer got a rise out of him. Just one more thing to avoid. One more thing to complain about bitterly when he was finally old enough to retire and could write his memoirs.

Or so Sunli told himself. He didn't know what would happen when Kinaki died. Would Wanho take over? Or would the land divest itself of the pair of them and settle on someone else's shoulders?

And what would happen to the demons then? Would Sunli survive? Would any of them?

He hadn't cooperated with his demon. Not much. He'd just asked to *see*. That ability had helped them at first, as Sunli was easily able to direct them around the more dangerous vegetation, as well as the holes that continued to materialize out of nowhere, deep crevices designed to not merely cause someone to fall, but to hold them there.

The land had turned cruel.

They were nearing the border, though. They'd gone directly east when they'd set off, hoping to make their way around the massive army fighting at the border. Only for the last few days had they turned north.

Chaotu had been impatient, of course. He hadn't understood the need for such concealment.

He didn't understand that they needed to cross the border unseen. There was no reason to believe that Unnir's warriors wouldn't kill them on the spot.

After they'd crossed the border, and found someplace safe to hole up, they could send one of the warriors to go bargain or something. Arrange for safe passage.

Sunli's legs were shaking by the time he got to the top of the latest damned hill. Fortunately, the others appeared to be resting in the shade of some massive boulders just past the crest. He limped his way over and collapsed. The rock felt nice and cool against his sweating back. He closed his eyes for a moment, intending to fully relax.

Deadly darkness greeted him, full of sharp teeth and claws.

He sprang back up, away from the rocks with a startled shriek. The others had also risen, the guards with their swords.

"What is it?" Lijun asked softly. She slowly walked over to him, as if afraid he would run away. Or possibly mindlessly attack.

Sunli gulped. "There's danger in the shadows," he said. He peered closer at the rocks. "The rocks—they're unbalanced. The ground behind is hollow. Putting your weight on them would spring the trap."

"I don't see any trap," Chaotu scorned.

Sunli knew that it wasn't fully his will that moved his body forward, that lent him the strength to push on the rock, to freeze him solidly into place as it slid backwards, crashing with a loud thump into the crevice that opened up behind it.

"Oh," Chaotu said after a moment.

Sunli shivered, suddenly cold. "Stay out in the open," he said, his voice harsh as he fought to push out the words past Belam's control. "There will be more traps ahead."

"Thank you," Lijun said softly after Chaotu and the guards had walked away, plotting out their next camp.

Sunli shrugged. "It's why you brought me along," he said honestly. He knew that the others didn't care for him. They only saw him as corrupted. A lesser evil, perhaps, but still evil. They did not have Lijun's faith that a person could both be part of the underworld as well as try to live a good life. Could have a demon riding him and still try to do the right thing.

It wasn't until later that evening, after the sun had gone down and cold shadows filled the earth, that Belam would speak directly to him. At first, it had been mostly whining about no longer being in the city, but more recently, his tactics had changed.

You know you think you're doing good, trying to save Kinaki's heirs. What if you're just leading them into another trap?

If we can get a message to Unnir, she will treat with them fairly, Sunli insisted.

Why not kill them on sight? Or worse, treat them like the traitors they are.

Sunli sighed and turned over again on his cot. It was marvelously lightweight. Just a touch of magic assembled it, made it as comfortable a spot as he was going to get out here in the wilderness.

Normally, Sunli would agree with that doubting voice in his head. Kinaki's heirs would be viewed with suspicion.

These weren't normal times, however. He doubted that

Unnir, who had seen the true nature of the LandHolder, would turn them away. No, she had a softer heart than her uncle, the previous LandHolder.

Hopefully that would not ultimately be her undoing.

ALL OF THEM could sense the nearby border. Sunli didn't know how the others would describe it. He thought of the differences between the two lands as the divide between turbulence and calm.

Although if he was also being completely honest, the lands controlled by the House of Gold were less lively, almost dull in comparison to where he stood.

Looking out across that invisible line filled Sunli with a dread that Belam didn't have to add to. While the air no longer tasted sweet in the lands of the House of Cobalt, he was afraid that he'd drown on the other side of the border.

They stood on a sloped hillside—of course, the area couldn't possibly smooth out and make it easy for them. Giant pine trees stood guard along the border, bristling with sharp needles, as if ready to catch any ill-doer. The ground beneath them was spongy and awkward to walk across, as they sank in the earth unpredictably.

All Sunli smelled was smoke. He missed the scent of the pines.

Would he ever be able to smell it again?

The setting sun amplified the creaks and groans of the nearby trees, bringing the woods to an eerie half-life. The wind couldn't seem to make up its mind, alternately pushing them forward or holding them back.

The group had agreed that the two warriors should cross the border first, followed by the two young people. Sunli had insisted on going last, not only because he was slower than the others, but because the land in front of him made his soul tremble with the same horrible fear he'd felt when he'd first been granted the ability to *see*.

The warriors slipped over the border without an issue. However, Sunli found himself holding his breath, sweating inappropriately, until both Chaotu and Lijun crossed over as well.

Now, it was his turn.

Sunli swallowed around the dry lump in his throat. He found himself gasping as he drew closer, as if the air had suddenly thinned. His vision darkened. He pushed his feet forward, one step at a time. His legs shook and his head pounded.

He would make it across that border if it was the last thing he did.

Finally, Sunli crossed that invisible line. He kept going out of momentum, despite how the land pushed back at him.

There was no welcoming force for him here. The land did not want his kind.

Sunli nearly turned back immediately. But he didn't want Lijun to think he was abandoning her. He stumbled forward. He raised his hand to wave at them.

Wait. What had happened to his hand? Why was the flesh so blackened and hardened? Even under the dark cover of the trees he could tell that he'd changed, his nails turned into claws.

By the Granite Tombs! What had happened to him?

He tried to say something to the group, but all that came out was a creaking growl.

The land pushed back at him harshly. He stumbled again.

A bright point of pain blossomed in his shoulder. He howled, surprised, and stumbled backwards.

A second momentary flash of agony suffused his ribs.

He looked down, the searing pain slowing everything around him.

Why were there arrows sticking out of him?

He swung around, seeking his enemies. He tried to tell them to wait, to stop, he wasn't a monster. He was there to *help* the heirs of Kinaki. He was no spy or saboteur!

The final shot landed in his throat, cutting off his breath. He fell slowly to his back, blinking in time with his slowing heartbeat.

He thought he saw Lijun leaning over him. She had such a soft glow to her. He would have gladly guided her and been a part of her life forever.

Then Belam stole away all his sight, as well as his soul, and he slid into the underworld and knew no more.

Chapter Twenty-Three

HOUSE OF GOLD

VIDE SAT in his tent and listened to the report being provided by his brother's companion in arms, Eynolfa. His glass of wine sat half-full on the table in front of him—he wasn't actually drinking much, anymore. The glass and the wine were as much of a habit as anything else, to give his hands something to do. Because he wasn't about to give into the urge to drum his fingers on the table, as much as he wanted to.

The woman in front of him was tough—tougher than most, truth be told. The skin on her long face was red from the heat and sunlight, though her anger might have something to do with that as well. She'd changed out of her armor and wore a long, loose robe, as did most of the warriors in camp when they were out of their gear. Hers happened to be a pale green, accenting her emerald eyes. Which were practically sparking.

"I know that some of the VeinHolders held your brother in disregard, initially," Eynolfa concluded. "But he no longer has to prove himself as he once did. His recklessness...

Honestly, he will kill more than he saves. If someone doesn't have a word with him."

She gave him a significant Look at that.

Vide grimly nodded. "Thank you," he said with a heavy sigh. "I have spoken with him before. I will speak with him again."

Eynolfa gave him a sharp nod, turned on her heel, and marched out the door.

Vide found himself reaching for his glass, intending to slam back the wine. He hesitated with the glass halfway to his lips.

He didn't want to dull his wits, not even the least, before he went to speak with his brother. Again.

Though honestly, with Emil, he'd never needed to be fully armed. Emil was a follower, not a leader. A do-er, not a thinker.

At least before the war. Now, he was turning into the worst of both, trying to be a leader but still not thinking.

Vide put his wine glass back on the table and stood. His own quarters were spartan, particularly compared to how he'd formerly lived. The brown, canvas tent was maybe seven-foot square. The cot that was long enough to fit his lanky frame was shoved against the far wall. A sturdy wooden table and two chairs took up most of the rest of the space. Books, maps, notes were piled high on the table, as Vide sometimes did his best thinking on paper.

The grass underneath was well trampled but he'd never bothered to conjure up rugs to hide it. A few robes hung on a pole next to the open tent flap, but no holder for armor or weapons. He had no need for armor. He'd trained to use a sword and shield, but that had never been where either his skills or his interest laid.

Vide wasn't sure what he was going to say to Emil. They'd had this argument more than once. Seemed that his dear brother needed to be reminded once again that the pair of them had *plans* for after this godforsaken war.

Although Vide's plans had continued to change and evolve.

He almost, *almost* had come to respect Unnir. She had the capacity to learn, which honestly, had surprised him. It was about the highest compliment he could think of. She was making faster, better decisions.

Of course, she'd been relying on him for much of her strategy in terms of the war. He would grudgingly admit that she'd come up with a few things on her own, such as staggering the warriors between battles so the demons they fought had never grown used to who they were fighting against, could never learn a pattern to the fighting.

Unnir might possibly be tolerable as LandHolder once this was all over. But only as long as she made him a Holder in his own right, so that he no longer had to see her, or quite frankly, anyone on a regular basis.

He'd had a daydream recently of having the time to write the history of the land. Just to sit alone with his thoughts and his books and his papers. Maybe a true history of the war, with all the mistakes as well as all the brilliant decisions he'd made.

He'd spend the evening reading the best phrases that he'd come up with to Emil. When his brother wasn't being an idiot, of course.

Vide strode out of his tent and walked directly to Emil's. His brother's tent was larger than his own, made out of a brighter canvas to allow more light in. It also reflected his rank better, being higher now that the VeinHolders had come to regard him as an equal.

No guard stood outside the tent. While there was no need—Emil was more than capable of taking care of himself—Vide still disapproved. There should be someone to turn away sycophants and those who would bother Emil when he was resting.

That Vide didn't have a guard didn't matter. He needed to be accessible, so that any messengers with news of a battle could reach him.

He pushed the tent flap to the side and cautiously stuck his head in.

Emil sat at the table, toying with the glass of wine in his hand. His armor was on its holder, already cleaned from the day's gore and polished, looking like new. Emil himself was clean as well, his blond hair neatly tied back, wearing a dark gray robe that suited him.

He yawned mightily, tilting his head back and opening his mouth so wide Vide was surprised his jaw didn't crack. Then he dropped his head back down.

"You just going to stand there staring daggers?" Emil growled. "Or come in and actually yell at me?"

Vide walked over and sat on the other chair. He didn't bother conjuring up a glass for himself. "You know that I'm not the only one who thought you took too great of a risk today," he started off with. He didn't try to keep the scolding tone out of his voice.

"I know," Emil said. He sighed. "But rushing that group of demons was the only way to save those warriors. And besides, we only lost five out of the group. Instead of the dozens of fighters."

A group of warriors had been isolated on the battlefield, cut off and surrounded by the fiercest of demons. Instead of allowing them all to die, Emil gathered a band of warriors to himself and broke through the line.

"You could have designated one of your own commanders to lead the charge," Vide pointed out. "You didn't have to do it yourself."

Emil sighed. Vide could tell his brother wanted to argue with him. He tried to gentle his voice.

"The other VeinHolders look up to you now," Vide said. "You don't have to continue proving yourself this way."

Emil's head shot up.

Maybe Vide's tone hadn't been as gentle as he'd planned.

"You're wrong," Emil said. "I do, and I will continue to need to prove myself to them." He held up his hand when Vide would have jumped in. "Yes, I've earned their respect. I know that. I'm not a complete idiot, no matter what you may think."

Vide prudently decided not to try to say anything. Emil would always be a complete idiot, particularly when compared to Vide.

"But that respect is grudging. Tenuous. Every time I make a mistake, it slips. It will take years for me to undo the damage from earlier," Emil said.

After a long moment's pause, Vide finally said, "Can I say something now? Is it my turn, yet?"

Emil rolled his eyes. "Not as if I could stop you," he muttered.

"Why is it so important? What others think of you? You've never cared before. We have only tried to curry favor to accomplish our bigger plans. Not because we actually wanted to be popular." Vide found himself speaking more from the heart than he'd planned. "What are you hoping to gain by retaining their regard?"

Did Emil actually have some plan that he'd forgotten to tell Vide about? Some scheme that was sure to fail without his brother's help?

He hadn't expected Emil to sit there, gaping at him like a landed fish, before finally, shaking his head and softly chuckling.

"You know, I'd forgotten what we used to be like," Emil

said. "Always scheming. Always seeking tit for tat. Building up an endless list of favors." He took a sip of his wine. "Fighting is based on merit. Training. Discipline."

"And magic and power," Vide pointed out. "Which falls more to the rich families than the poor." Surely his brother wasn't thinking that they all were equal or some such nonsense.

"True," Emil granted, nodding. "Though there are always exceptions. But you have to rely on the warriors around you. It isn't a solo act. It can't be. Not in the sorts of battles we're fighting. We look out for each other. Warriors in arms. That sort of thing."

"And your point being?" Vide asked. "Unless you're too tired and drunk to have one."

"As I said before, I've become responsible," Emil said. "A leader. I'd like to keep that title, at least in the minds of the warriors. Which means yes, I'm going to do stupid things like I did today, to save the lives of my warriors. Whether you or anyone else likes it or not."

Vide nodded. He wasn't disappointed as much as melancholy.

The old days of their youth, causing troubles for the LandHolder, were so far in the past that he could barely remember them. But he still fell into his old ways of thinking. He couldn't help it.

If he was honest with himself, he no longer really wished Unnir harm. Not anymore. He understood now why the land had chosen her, and neither Emil or himself.

She *cared*. And so the land, in return, cared for them.

If she died now, it wouldn't surprise him in the least if the land now settled on Emil's broad shoulders.

He'd been infected with that *caring* as well.

They weren't who they had once been. The change had

happened some time before, hence the melancholy as opposed to pure sadness.

"What, no quick snip or angry rebuttal?" Emil asked with a soft smile.

"The future is new," Vide admitted. "Just as there is no augury, not really anymore. I cannot see what will come of us after the war." He paused, then glared at Emil. "Because you *will* make it until after the war."

"I can't promise you that," Emil said softly. "As much as I'd like to."

"Are we losing?" Vide asked. It had never occurred to him that they wouldn't at some point be able to completely push Kinaki back.

"We're in a holding pattern," Emil said. "Equal losses and gains on both sides."

Vide nodded. "When will the tipping point come?"

"I don't know," Emil said, shrugging. He suddenly yawned again. "I'm sorry. I need to go sleep now. So I can get up in the morning and do something stupid again."

"Of course," Vide said. "I wouldn't expect anything less of you."

Back alone in his own tent, Vide felt true sadness wrap around him. Yes, he had his dreams of maybe sitting and writing someday. But only if Emil was there with him.

He'd never found a partner. The women he'd been with were just too tiresome, in the long term. They all seemed to want something from him, something he would never be able to give them. The few men he'd been with hadn't been much better.

The only person he'd ever been able to tolerate for any amount of time had been his brother. Vide had never needed anyone else.

And if this war took Emil from him…Vide knew he'd never heal.

Chapter Twenty-Four

HOUSE OF PEARL

꧁꧂

DARIKUTO SAT UNDER A PAVILION, taking his midday break blessedly alone. He sat on a rug that had been brought for this purpose, not needing either tables or chairs. The ground was good enough for him. The army was spread out before him, mostly visible by the holes they made in the tall grass, which, fortunately, had turned out to be less bloodthirsty than the forests. The air carried the smell of too many warriors who needed baths and the constant scent of baking dirt.

His people needed a rest. This land drained them with every step. He knew he couldn't put off doing the spell to take on the mantle of the lands of the House of Crystal for much longer. He'd been hoping that spending more time there would acclimate him to the lands, and the lands to him.

However, these lands remained aloof and foreign.

He understood the casual foothills and low mountains that made up the eastern border of his lands. He didn't have a feeling for the towering peaks that demarcated the northern border of these lands. Those mountains were impassible: not merely because of their height and frozen nature, but because they had their own awareness. In many ways, they were their own Land and jealous of their borders. No mere LandHolder had ever held them, or ever would, as far as they were concerned.

They guarded their territory as fiercely as Chuyoko guarded him. She continued to do what she thought best, regardless of whatever order he gave. He knew she was still fanatically bound to him. Eventually, that devotion would slip.

The Plan had called for him to ride into the House of Crystal lands like a savior. He had expected to be welcomed, not just by the people there but by the land itself.

He hadn't expected the land to attack, for warriors from the House of Crystal to harry them and pick off his own warriors when they could.

Shimokoro was no help either. He had no augury, no ability to predict the perfect place or time for Darikuto to cast his spells. Darikuto hadn't been able to rely on augury for a while either. He still would have liked to choose the most auspicious place for his ascension.

However, looking out over the endless, featureless fields, one place looked just as good, or as bad, as another.

Summer still clasped them in her powerful hand. The grass never browned or yellowed, though. Darikuto wasn't sure why. Was there actually enough water under ground for the grass to find? Or was it because he and his army were in the area, and the land kept a level of awareness here, which kept everything fresh and green?

The warriors had to rely on stumbling across streams, as they couldn't use their magic to lead them to water, or to draw it to them. (The poor fool who'd tried to draw up some water from the ground had at first been tossed into the air by a geyser, then, after it abruptly vanished, was swallowed whole and alive. They heard his screams under the earth for a while before they were suddenly cut off.)

Darikuto had declared a midday break in their endless trudging across the grass. Everyone was hot and sticky. Bugs that normally could have been blown to the side plagued them, both with their whining wings as well as their stinging bites. The army had come across a miraculously intact herd of cattle. They still had salted, dried meat from that, though not much remained of their initial stores of food.

He knew he needed to get up. To start moving again. But he stayed where he was, meditating on where they were, where they were going.

A great longing for his own land overwhelmed him—the feel of shifting waters, the mountains at his back and the endless horizon in front of him. Oh, how he yearned to sink his feet deeply into earth that recognized him, was grateful for him! He found himself leaning to his left, toward the west, where his home lay.

Enough. He pushed himself upright. No more delays. The Plan wouldn't reach its glorious conclusion if he dallied any longer, filled with doubt.

He would never find the perfect location to cast his spell. He was going to have to fight for this land, to grasp it with strong, angry hands until it gave in and obeyed him.

He turned to the servant standing silently at the edge of the pavilion, probably grateful for the shade as well.

"Tell Shimokoro it's time," Darikuto announced.

The young girl's eyes grew wide before she hurried off.

Yes. It was time to claim this land as its proper owner.

So he could finally return home.

IT TOOK the rest of the day to prepare for the ceremony. Darikuto first cleansed himself as best he could. He'd hoped they'd have a river that he could dip into, but made do with water carried from one of the nearby streams.

In his own lands, Darikuto would have stepped into the ocean herself, possibly during a storm, asking for the goddess Morta to bless his endeavor. But this land was not as concerned with rivers and streams. No, it was filled with grasslands and far scattered trees.

Woods that they'd never dared go into, as even the slowly moving roots and branches could be treacherous.

After the cleansing, Darikuto dressed in robes that had been carried with them just for this occasion. They were heavy, covered in long ropes of pearls of every color: white, pink, silver, brown, green, blue, red, gold, purple, and of course, black. Strands of seed pearls hung from his sleeves, clicking softly when he moved. The material of the robe itself was also magnificent, woven from dark blue and black stripes. The stiff collar, cuffs, and plaques down the front were encrusted with abalone shells that glistened in the candlelight. The robe hung loosely from his shoulders, down to the ground where tiny bits of ochre coral were sewn.

Darikuto was one of the few who could still reliably call on the slightest of magic. Nothing too difficult, or his hold would snap and the magic would dangerously run loose.

The ceremony had started with the priests and priestesses who had accompanied the army, as well as the BlackPearlHolders, all crowded in underneath his pavilion. As dusk approached, Darikuto had lit all the candles surrounding him with a single glance, causing his audience to gasp.

It was as if they'd forgotten how easy magic had at one time been for all of them.

Darikuto understood that his magic was still coming

from his own lands, and not from this location. Maybe he should have paused just inside the border, where his own magic was the strongest, and done his spell there?

No, there would have been too much of the land that wouldn't have responded to him. He would have only been able to tear away a chunk of it. The rest would have broken off and grown wild, possibly as untamable as the mountains to the north.

It was better here. He would succeed. Every other part of The Plan had been accomplished. He could do this part as well.

Darikuto knew he was procrastinating. Doubt had taken hold in his mind. He needed to banish it before he started, or the spell would be doomed to fail.

He stepped away from Shimokoro and the others, leaving them standing beneath the pavilion. The army was spread out before him, though he couldn't really see the faces of the warriors, just felt their presence, knew their breath would carry him forward.

In the end, Darikuto had decided that he needed to face the north while casting his spell. That was where the true seat of this land's power lay. Despite the flat lands and hearty trees, the House of Crystal was aptly named. The primary source of power for this land lay in its crystals, and the crystals came from those mountains.

He'd never before reflected on the ocean and the pearls that were his own power and calling, but now he recognized it.

Darikuto had long ago memorized the prayers and poems that were supposedly needed to prepare the land for his holding. He let his voice soar out into the night, reciting the many deeds of his people, the glory of the land itself, and why they needed to join together.

Without meaning to, Darikuto reached for his magic to

sustain him. He found his roots sinking deep into the surrounding earth, down into the bedrock, where the two lands might be joined.

Excited, he continued on, his voice rising above the shrill cries of the nearby cicadas. Harsh winds directly from the mountains rushed at him, as if trying to blow away his words, stop the spell.

But the winds spread his words further, spinning his spell across more of the land.

He continued with his litany of praise. He couldn't stop, even as he felt himself growing weaker. The land was starting to respond to him. He could feel its awareness focus on him, not just the army surrounding him.

It wouldn't be long, now.

He wouldn't allow himself to rush, though. Just as every part of The Plan needed to come to fruition in its own time, so would this land come to him.

Already, he was starting to feel the power of this place seep into him. Soon, this land would sustain him as well as his own did.

It just took patience.

And an audacious Plan.

Chapter Twenty-Five

HOUSE OF CRYSTAL

BEFERY WAS grateful that they'd final made it to Holder Sitre's stronghold. While Akalina went to find Yimifut, Befery, always practical, took care of their things.

They'd been given a room in the main house, with two beds. Befery stood before the warmed stones of the hearth. Despite how warm the summer weather was outside, the hold seemed cold to her, as if the stones held the ice from the mountains.

She would never say anything about it to Akalina, as she was certain her sister wouldn't notice. And she wouldn't dream of speculating why the main house of the Hold was so cold. Holder Sitre had greeted them kindly and done everything she could to make them feel at home.

But still—the household was cold, and would always remain so. No amount of warmed rocks or hearths would change that fact in any household that Sitre ran.

Akalina came slamming through the door just after Befery had gotten settled in. "That idiot won't take the land!" she said. She didn't bother looking around the room, or noting that Befery had taken care of everything, put everything away.

Always the practical one.

"Why won't he?" Befery asked, sinking down into one of the comfortable chairs lined up perfectly in front of the heated stones.

"He wants to know *why*," Akalina said. She rolled her eyes. "Why can't he just take the land and figure that out later?"

"Why what?" Befery said cautiously, not wanting to draw Akalina's ire to herself, but still wanting to understand.

"Why the land chose him," Akalina said. She collapsed into the chair beside her sister, and stared at the heated rocks, as if daring them to try to warm her. "I kind of get it," she admitted quietly. "The land chose me because of my connection to the ghosts."

"And he doesn't have that sort of connection, I take it?" Befery asked.

Akalina shook her head. "He needs to take hold of the land. Soon. Before it grows too wild to be tamed."

Befery shrugged. "Couldn't someone else take it then? Draw the lines of wild power to them?"

Akalina looked at her sister with surprise. "What had you heard?" she demanded.

"There are rumors, you know," Befery said. She'd chatted with the servants as they'd aired out their room. "That once the land has been turned away from its intended Holder, that anyone with enough magic could draw it to them."

Akalina shrugged. "I don't know if it works that way. I'm not sure anyone does."

"Maybe Unnir will take the lands, then," Befery said.

"No, she's fighting a war with Kinaki," Akalina said firmly. "I know because the ghosts told me," she added after a moment.

"Darikuto?" Befery said.

Akalina pressed her lips together in a thin line and furrowed her brow. "I don't like him. And Ibitsima didn't trust him. Not one bit. It has to be Yimifut. He has to take the land."

"Or?" Befery asked after a moment.

Akalina turned her face toward her sister.

Funny, Befery hadn't ever really noticed just how large Akalina's eyes were in her face, how they appeared to suck in all the light. They were like holes of darkness sometimes, distant places where the ghosts hid.

"Or believe me, we are all doomed."

BEFERY WASN'T certain why Yimifut looked so shocked when they were introduced. Surely he'd seen her before, in his visions, right?

Akalina had told her, on the trip there, how Yimifut had predicted that she would be the only one left alive. He'd known that Ibitsima and the others would all be killed.

But all through the dinner held in their honor, Yimifut kept sneaking glances at Befery, as if trying to figure out why she was there.

The dinner wasn't anything fancy, just a good, hearty stew made from goat meat and root vegetables, and served with a delightful mead sweetened with fresh blackberries. Befery and Akalina sat near the head of the table with Sitre and her husband. At the far end of the table, the LandHolder's married children sat, with their children. Befery had to grin at the barely organized chaos the meal threatened to descend into more than once as the children started telling their stories.

After the meal, while Akalina and the LandHolder talked

their Important Business, Befery followed the children to their play area, and ended up sitting in front of the rocks of the heated hearth telling stories to each other.

Yimifut found her there, sitting on the floor, a little one in her lap nodding off, while three others played quietly in the corner for the time being.

"You don't have to do that, you know," Yimifut told her as he squatted down. He kept his voice low, so as not to wake the little girl. He was dressed in browns and greens, looking more like he came from the woods than from the solid stones of the Hold. His curly black hair had been cut so short it was just wavy, though Befery suspected that when he let it grow, it would mass out like a mane around his head. He looked at her with cool gray eyes that appeared to see right through her.

"I know," Befery said. "I miss my own children though. So it's been nice to be around them."

Yimifut nodded thoughtfully as he studied her.

"What do you see?" Befery asked after a few moments.

"What did Akalina tell you about what I see?" Yimifut said instead of answering.

"She said that you see the future, that you knew about Ibitsima's death long before it happened," Befery said.

"And?" Yimifut prompted when Befery didn't continue.

"And that you said she wore a white cloak around her shoulders. She always wondered if you saw that because of her connection to the ghosts," Befery continued.

Yimifut gave her a warm smile.

Befery realized it was one of the first she'd seen from the serious young man.

"I see auras, yes," Yimifut said. "I didn't understand them at first, what the colors meant. Yours is golden. Warm. With red tones."

Befery nodded. "I am the one who takes care of others," she said.

"More than that," Yimifut said. He paused, appearing to choose his words. "You carry the warmth of the hearth with you. Sitre is not as warm."

"Huh," Befery said, "imagine that!" As if she hadn't figured out that Holder Sitre was, in essence, cold.

Yimifut gave her another smile, as if he understood that he wasn't sharing any secret with her.

"You appeared to look at me with surprise, earlier," Befery finally said as she shifted the deadweight of the girl in her arms to a more comfortable position.

Yimifut nodded. "I'd never seen you before," he admitted. "I knew that Akalina would return, that I would see her again. But I always thought she was alone. I had never imagined that she would travel with her sister. With *you*."

"Why is that important?" Befery said. "We all know that augury isn't always accurate. We still have our own paths to make."

"True," Yimifut said. "I still can't imagine why you never appeared before."

"I don't know," Befery said. "Possibly because I'm not the important one. Akalina is." She was the one with a Destiny, the one the ghosts chose, the one who'd almost become a LandHolder.

"You are important, or you wouldn't be here," Yimifut said seriously.

Befery shrugged. "It doesn't matter. I don't have to be important. What matters is that I bring good people into the world, to carry on after me."

Befery could tell that Yimifut wanted to argue with her about the point, but then he let it pass.

"You're the practical one, yes?" he said after a moment.

Befery couldn't help her snort. "Akalina isn't always the most practical, that's true." There had been so many times on their journey that Akalina had turned to Befery for help when magic, bravado, and anger weren't the solution.

"So tell me, O practical one, what do you see when you look at me?" Yimifut asked.

Befery knew they had finally reached the crux of the evening. Akalina had said that Yimifut wouldn't agree to become the LandHolder until he understood why the land had chosen him.

"I see a very serious young man," Befery said. "And people have probably told you your entire life that you were born with an old soul, right?"

Yimifut nodded solemnly.

"My oldest, Tesitafi, is like that. At first I thought she was scared, but she isn't. She's cautious. Once she makes a decision, that's it. She sticks with her choice, no matter the consequences."

Befery paused, hoping that she was getting through to Yimifut. "So what I see before me is someone who struggles to make the right choice. Then, he will do whatever is necessary to do the right thing. Tesitafi had a favorite doll. But because it was her favorite, it became her youngest sister's favorite as well. They fought over it constantly. I finally had to intervene. Tesitafi chose to give up the doll, as she was growing out of such things anyway, and to give it to her sister. It was the right thing to do, despite the personal cost.

"And that is what I think you will do. You will take your time to choose the right path, then will stick with it, regardless of the price."

Befery took a deep breath, then shook her head. "But look at me! Rattling on to someone who might be the next LandHolder."

Yimifut gave her a bittersweet smile, that held as much

joy as sorrow. "But you're correct. And that is why the Land chose me. Because I *will* do the right thing, no matter what."

Yimifut stood and stretched out his arms.

Befery couldn't see the magic happen. She felt it, however. Something cold entered the room, like a storm cloud, bringing fresh fall rain and the smell of snow from the mountains. It swirled around once, twice, before it rushed at Yimifut.

Yimifut braced to accept the Land, steadying himself as it descended. His brown pants and vest shaded closer to black, while the green of his shirt brightened to the color of new maple leaves. His gray eyes faded, the whites of his eyes more prominent. Despite its shortness, his black hair stood up and lengthened, curls replacing the waves.

The little girl in Befery's lap shifted, then gave a happy sigh, a smile creeping across her face.

The land had its LandHolder again.

Peace settled into Befery's bones. She felt magic creeping back as well.

Her joy was short-lived.

A terrible, stormy expression crossed Yimifut's face.

"Darikuto is trying to steal the land from me," he announced. "I will not have it."

With that, he disappeared, leaving cold winds behind.

Befery shivered. It appeared that Yimifut might have made his decision too late, if he now had to go and fight another LandHolder for possession of his land.

When Befery went to let Akalina know what had happened, she couldn't find her sister anywhere.

It seemed that she, too, had been taken by the LandHolder to go fight Darikuto. Along with what few warriors had been at the Hold.

Befery sat vigil with the rest of the family, waiting until the dawn to find out their fate.

Chapter Twenty-Six
HOUSE OF COBALT

THE BODY that Wanho had to constantly support chafed him. His spirit was greater than this mortal form! He longed to burst out of it, to uncoil his massive body, to rise up to his full height, towering above all those on the battlefield before him.

Let them know fear of his true form.

But he couldn't leave Kinaki behind. Without that mortal body, he had no access to the land of the living.

If he could only figure out a way to break apart from Kinaki, but still live!

Then, he could truly become a god, here in the world of the living. Oh, the stories they would tell about him! The temples and feasts they would dedicate to him! The swirling dances and piles of bodies, all for him!

He wondered now and again why the gods had not come down and smitten him for his presumption, for not just leaving the underworld, but for carrying it with him, up onto the land of the living. The Goddess Morta herself had set his task for him, to test those of the living who passed into the underworld. Why did she continue to ignore him?

The fact that he existed meant that the gods existed, right? He hadn't been born merely out of the imagination of the living.

There must be something he could do about his current situation, though. Some way of carrying Kinaki down into the underworld and stashing his body there, so that Wanho could truly reign over the land of the living.

Wanho had tried denying the mortal body. Tried to not eat and not sleep. Though he could push the limits of Kinaki's endurance, eventually, the body always held sway. Neither Kinaki nor Wanho could completely control it.

Then he'd tried locking Kinaki away. Slowly, subtly, or at least as subtle as a demon could be, Wanho pushed Kinaki to the side, whispering in his ear constantly, things the living didn't really hear but still acted upon.

Still, Kinaki maintained his independence. He insisted on doing his warrior stretches every morning, a time that left Wanho in a stupor. Kinaki made decisions without Wanho, or refused to do things like calling in the other troops who were still fighting the barbarians to the south. He insisted that he was still committed to the war, but Wanho had his doubts.

Soon, though, it would be time to put Kinaki to the test. He would have to prove his loyalty. They were coming up to a terrible crossroads. Wanho knew the time was coming. He had no augury or foretelling abilities. He still read it in the wind and the blood mingled with the mud.

The time of Great Pain was coming soon.

And Kinaki would either welcome and relish it, or they'd both be dead.

Chapter Twenty-Seven

HOUSE OF GOLD

UNNIR FOUND it strange that she actually missed holding court some days. Maybe because she felt more isolated from her decisions. The consequences in court were just as important, but she would have time, if she made the wrong decision, to correct her course.

Here, if she chose wrong, she'd lose warriors later that day. Good people, good fighters.

Currently, she was faced with a dilemma that she didn't know how to resolve. She'd never been faced with such a choice before.

Frankly, she didn't think anyone had.

Chaotu and Lijun, Kinaki's children, had been brought by Torja and some of the warriors into the main camp. Torja had been granted a vision, telling her that something of value was coming into the lands of the House of Gold.

This meant that Unnir couldn't throw these two away, or just kill them. Torja had assured Unnir that they weren't spies.

They'd rested and were now on their way to Unnir's tent. Unnir had put two additional chairs and a table in the center of the wide open space. A bottle of some of her finest wine stood on the table with three cups, along with a beautiful glass pitcher filled with clear water and matching glasses. A silver platter filled with soft cheese, grapes, and fresh bread completed the preparations.

Unnir had changed into one of the two good robes that she'd brought. It was dark green with the traditional long sleeves that she always found so elegant. She wore her blonde hair in braids tight against the sides of her head. She knew they made her look severe. She didn't care.

After she'd shuffled from one foot to the other for the third time, Unnir made took a deep breath, telling herself to stop being ridiculous. She shouldn't be nervous. She'd greeted foreign dignities before. But always in her court, sitting on her grand honey locust throne.

A pang of sorrow struck her heart hard. She missed that throne. Missed the court. Missed her old life, even if she'd been constantly fighting with her cousins as well as most of the Holders.

Things would be different when the battles were over. She wasn't about to put up with any more of their petty bickering.

That was something else the war had taught her: what was actually important, as well as what wasn't.

One of the guards outside opened the tent flap, allowing Chaotu and Lijun into the space.

Unnir had met them previously, when the House of Gold had hosted the annual gathering of the LandHolders. They'd both aged considerably over the last year or so. Or perhaps that was just another symptom of these times.

Chaotu had the same straight black hair as did most of the people from the House of Cobalt, and was short like them as well, barely coming up to her chin. His dark eyes looked haunted and his face pinched, the sharp nose and chin jutting with disapproval. He wore a brown shirt and trousers instead of the traditional blue robes of his household.

Lijun looked like a pale version of her brother, her long black hair bound up in a practical single braid down her back. She stood two inches shorter than he. Sorrow filled her features, her red lips downturned and her eyes glassy. It looked as though she'd borrowed a robe from someone of the House of Gold. It was a delicate light green, and three times too big for her.

"I welcome you to the lands of the House of Gold," Unnir said stiffly. "Please, come, sit, and enjoy a slight repast as we talk. I'm sorry I can't offer you more."

Lijun suddenly smiled at her. It was quite remarkable how much different she looked. She no longer looked like a tragic heroine about to take her own life, but instead, more like a Holder's daughter, someone of importance and power.

"Thank you for taking us in, like the two orphans we are. Your hospitality is more than generous," Lijun said. "Please, may I serve you? What would you prefer?"

Unnir nearly stopped herself, but then didn't bother to. She snorted loudly in laughter at the girl, who looked started at eliciting such a response.

"We are all adults here. Serve yourselves," Unnir stated plainly as she took her seat.

Lijun blinked in surprise at the LandHolder sitting before her guests. She opened and closed her mouth but didn't say anything, and instead, meekly took a chair.

Chaotu gave her a cool look of assessment before he gave her a sharp nod and sat himself.

The previous LandHolder, Yudur, had favored his sons over Unnir. Magic was a great leveler, and some of the strongest warriors and VeinHolders were women. However, Yudur had opened expressed his distaste for female leaders, and for the most part, didn't consider them as worthy as males.

Given how Lijun had just reacted, Unnir would bet that Kinaki had done the same, and had favored Chaotu as well as her male cousins over Lijun, expecting the females to just "serve" them.

Unnir hid her grin as she poured herself a glass of wine, then pushed the bottle toward the siblings.

They'd obviously been expecting something much more formal. That had been how the court of the House of Gold had always run.

Unnir couldn't be bothered with that currently.

"Tell me about your journey here," Unnir said, hoping to start off with something easier before they got to the more difficult topics.

Unfortunately, that appeared to be the wrong thing to ask. Lijun teared up again immediately.

Chaotu paused for a moment after he'd poured both himself and his sister a glass of delicate white wine. He put his hand on her shoulder for a moment, as if giving her comfort. Then he turned and directed his words at Unnir.

"We had a guide. The head of the Temple of Truth. Sunli. He'd been corrupted by a demon, but only a little bit."

Lijun looked as though she might protest, but then subsided.

"He could see the truth of things, the truth of the land we traveled across, the people we met. He could see straight into a person's soul," Chaotu continued. He took a sip of his wine, pausing again to really taste it.

Unnir knew that it was of the finest quality, light and delicate, fruity yet balanced. She was glad that he could appreciate it.

"But he still bore a demon," Chaotu said. He gave his sister a hard look. "He did everything he could to help us cross the lands of the House of Cobalt, seeing traps that we couldn't. The land there is so horribly corrupt. It hates us. All people."

Unnir found that fascinating. She remembered being there, feeling as though the ground was actually composed of ashes. Had it grown contemptuous, the longer the LandHolder was working with a demon?

He could never be allowed to take a single step across the border, into the lands of the House of Gold.

"So while he could see, he was also holding us back," Chaotu said. "The border clearly frightened him. We let him cross last. I wasn't even sure he would." He took on a grim expression, suddenly regaining the impression that he was much older. "Your guards killed him."

Unnir blinked. She had known that they'd killed someone who'd been following after the others. They'd watched him creeping along. They'd assumed that he was a demon sent to stop them.

Torja had also seen this demon in her vision. She was the one who'd warned the guards that he was approaching and that he needed to be killed.

"I can't apologize for what my guards did," Unnir said slowly. "He bore a demon. The head of the Temple of Truth had seen him in a vision, and knew that he had to die."

Both Lijun and Chaotu seemed surprised at that. Hadn't Torja told them? Or hadn't they asked? Surely the priestess would have seen them grieving, particularly the girl.

Had Torja become so focused on her augury that she could no longer see what was right in front of her?

"I am, however, truly sorry for your loss," Unnir said.

Lijun spoke, her voice soft and ragged. "He'd always been my friend, just like his predecessor." She took a sip of wine and cleared her throat. "Sunli claimed that Kinaki himself wanted us saved."

Chaotu made a face of disgust, obviously not agreeing with his sister.

"He did, and I believe him," Lijun said. "Believed him," she corrected herself a moment later.

"When did Kinaki tell Sunli that he wanted you saved?" Unnir asked, astonished. "It must have been before the demon came. Right?"

"No," Lijun said with a firm shake of her head. "He always did the exercises with the rest of the warriors, in the courtyard, every morning. Sunli said that Kinaki appeared to be more in control then, the demon asleep. He gestured once, as if cradling something precious in his arms. Like this," Lijun said, demonstrating.

"I see," Unnir said, though she really didn't. "And so Sunli read that to mean that Kinaki wanted the pair of you saved?"

"Yes," Chaotu said, nodding. "I'm not sure I believe it either," he added. "However, he arranged for me to be 'killed,' and the news brought to the LandHolder."

"Interesting," Unnir said. She broke off a chunk of bread and chewed it while she thought.

Chaotu followed her example, spreading some of the soft cheese on it. Lijun helped herself to a few grapes. They silently ate together.

Unnir kept going over what Chaotu and Lijun had told her, as well as her main, biggest question: what was she going to do with them?

Finally, she realized her mistake. While in the end, this was her decision, the two siblings were also adults. They could direct their own lives, at least to a certain extent.

"All right," Unnir said, trying to find the right words but then deciding they didn't matter. "What am I supposed to do with the pair of you?" The words finally said out loud, Unnir found more tumbling afterward. "What do you expect? Are you just here until the war ends and then you'll return to your own lands? Or are you here for good? Do you expect Kinaki to win? What would happen to you if he does? The Land won't settle on you if you're here, at least not according to legend. So what am I to do with you?"

Chaotu gave her the first warm smile she'd seen. "I've asked myself the same questions, multiple times," he said. "I continue to wonder if news of my survival would cause my father to crumble, or if he'd fight harder to get over here if he knew I was just across the border."

Unnir nodded. She'd been thinking along the same lines. Abruptly, she came to a decision.

"We will tell the LandHolder that you are here," she said after a few moments. "Yes. And here's how we'll do it."

Seemed that she had learned something from Vide after all.

Chapter Twenty-Eight

HOUSE OF PEARL

THE DREAM STARTED as it always did. Benitoyo sat in the windowless room in the Temple of Truth with Sunli. The soothing green walls held their own light. A beautiful painting of a window overlooking a garden filled one of the walls. They sat on low cushions, sipping a sweet jasmine tea, and talking of nothing substantial, how Benitoyo's latest trades had gone, or Sunli fretting over details of the coming celebration of the God Djediese.

It was a lovely memory. One of the reasons why the dream was so disturbing was because it always started to close to the truth, what had actually happened.

The lights in the room dimmed. It was as if clouds had gathered over the garden in the painted picture. But that was impossible. It was just a painting.

However, when Benitoyo looked, the blue sky that usually dominated the top part of the picture was now covered in light gray clouds that grew darker quickly. A storm was approaching.

He couldn't help but jump when lightning suddenly flashed from one black cloud to another. The beautiful

163

butterflies strained their wings helplessly against the storm winds. Rain slashed down, tearing petals from the flowers. For a moment, the paths through the garden all looked pretty, covered in red, blue, yellow, pink, and white petals. Then the rain poured down harder, turning the walkways to mud.

Benitoyo found it difficult to tear his eyes away. He didn't want to see the complete destruction of the garden. When the lightning struck the trees and a fire started to race through the woods at the back, Benitoyo was finally able to look away.

The sight in front of him filled him with just as much fear. Sunli still sat there, but his skin had grown both black and wizened. Claws made up his hands now, with sharp gray talons. His face remained much the same, except his eyes had changed, growing large and golden. They wept yellow, viscous tears, as if full of pus.

"I see you," Sunli growled out. "You obey a demon. Though you do not carry one. Yet."

Benitoyo felt tears streaming down his cheeks, the moisture hot against his cool skin.

"I'm sorry," he moaned. "I didn't mean to."

"All of us do what we must," Sunli said. "For what it's worth, I'm sorry as well."

Benitoyo wasn't sure what Sunli meant at first. Then the priest's jaw started to lengthen, his mouth turning into a snout. Sunli worked his jaw, moving the bottom part around in a grotesquely fascinating way. Sharp teeth shot out all along the long snout. Sunli continued to open and close his mouth, stretching, the snout growing larger and larger, until it took up most of his face. Tiny golden eyes peered out above it. It looked ridiculously huge, particularly when compared to the rest of his body.

Sunli appeared to topple forward, as if the weight of that

great snout had pulled him over, making him lose his balance.

Benitoyo immediately reached out to him, as if to help him up.

He recognized his mistake as soon as he touched Sunli.

The priest turned his head and casually, almost without thought, opened his jaws wide and swallowed Benitoyo's head down whole.

Benitoyo always woke at that part, as darkness descended and started to chill his soul.

In other dreams, Sunli had pulled Benitoyo to pieces with his sharp claws. Or had impaled his side with a large dagger, pinning him to the painting, and things from the garden had taken over Benitoyo's destruction.

Benitoyo lay shivering on his bed, trying to convince himself that it had all been a dream. He was safe now, here, still in the palace in Jinyi. Nothing had come after him, no demon was going to eat him alive.

The room looked much the same as always. A high chest of drawers in the corner holding almost all of his clothes. A writing desk in another corner, now closed and locked. The large bed he lay on, with the best of goose-feather mattresses, comfortable and warm. Clanging noises came through the window, as always, the cooks for the palace getting ready for the day.

The main difference was the large rucksack leaning next to the door, with Benitoyo's clothes and provisions. He didn't know if he could count on finding hospitality at any of the crossroad inns, so most of the pack was filled with dried meat and fruit.

While it would be nice to find a ride, he was prepared to walk all the way back to his wife if he had to.

Benitoyo had wanted to say goodbye in person to Sunli, but he hadn't been able to see the priest in a few days. An acolyte had always greeted Benitoyo warmly but let him know that Sunli was busy seeing someone else.

Too bad.

Something had happened to Sunli the night of the attack on Ibitsima and the other LandHolders. The few times they'd met, Sunli was always jumping, startled by things that Benitoyo couldn't see. And he spent a lot of time staring out into nothing, or worse, staring at people, as if he could read their souls.

Had Sunli been taken over by a demon? He didn't act like it. Benitoyo had seen the way that some of the warriors had changed, growing aggressive, demanding maggoty meat and acting like drunken braggarts, even when no liquor was to be found.

Sunli acted more like a man for whom the veils had been lifted. But he would never answer any of Benitoyo's oblique questions about it.

At first Benitoyo had been determined to stay in Jinyi, despite the horrible condition, the way the air smelled like ash now, the feeling that nothing remained solid, not the walls, not the earth.

But it was finally time for Benitoyo to leave. He'd learned everything that he could by staying here in Jinyi. The army was still divided. He had no idea for how long. He assumed that eventually Kinaki would call all his warriors to him. Only one half of the army fought along the border, seeking to break through into the lands of the House of Gold.

He feared for Unnir and the others. Did they realize that Kinaki had an entire second army ready to throw at them?

He would tell Unnir if he could.

For now, Benitoyo had decided the best place for him was back home. At least for a while. He could always come back to Jinyi after.

After what, exactly, he was never certain. But after

something had occurred. Something had changed. Something had swept through and cleaned up the land.

Benitoyo heard the kitchen staff banging pots and pans together, though they rarely ever cooked, now. They served slugs raw, and slimy weeds that still had dirt on the roots.

That was part of why Benitoyo felt he had to leave. Food was growing scarcer. The prices were outrageous as well.

Most of the stalls in the market were now empty. Farmers were staying out on their farms, away from the city, afraid of what would happen if they came in. They might or might not be able to sell anything that they'd harvested.

And everyone was afraid of being possessed by demons.

Benitoyo had never really prayed that often or that hard to the God Xiuma. He had an altar to the god set up, of course. Every merchant would hedge their bets that way. The god was carved out of good quality cobalt, his cheeks fat above the god's wide grin. Benitoyo had placed small pieces of raw gold, along with a few uncut gems at the feet of Xiuma, sitting on his throne.

Though Benitoyo had no idea when, or even if, he'd be returning, he'd left Xiuma's offerings where they were. It wouldn't pay for him to be stingy toward his god.

Anything to ensure that his god wasn't stingy with his protection of Benitoyo and his profits.

Benitoyo threw off the covers of the bed as he threw off the last remnants of the bad dream.

Soon, maybe in a month's time, he'd be in his own bed. Ozukshi would help keep all the nightmares away.

Or so Benitoyo told himself as he got himself ready for his journey.

Leaving the city was more treacherous than Benitoyo had anticipated. Guards stood along the edges of every road leading into or out of the city. Seemed that they didn't want people running away as they had been.

Or they were worried about spies. Benitoyo had never been able to get a straight answer.

The day was gray and cool, despite it being the height of summer. Every once in a while a gray or white flake floated down, ashes from somewhere. The sun was a mere orange ball, weak and defeated by the clouds.

Fortunately, Benitoyo knew a back way out of the city, cutting through a neighborhood that appeared deserted, then heading out across a field of tall wheat that should have been harvested weeks before.

The grass cut his hands to slivers before he realized how sharp the edges were. He had to slow his pace, as large holes appeared in the earth now and then, seemingly out of nowhere.

However, he didn't dare cross over to the road yet. There had been reports of robbers just outside the city. He spent the entire day going cross country, not seeing another soul.

That night, Benitoyo decided to make his camp, such as it was, beside a great tree. It was an ancient oak, mighty and proud. The grass underneath it was much shorter and mostly soft.

"Thank you for your protection," Benitoyo told the tree solemnly as he settled in for the evening. "And your excellent hospitality."

Though he didn't actually think the tree heard him, he still felt more comfortable as he settled in for the night.

Great winds sprang up as dark fell. Fortunately, they didn't carry rain. They tore at the tree. It kept him awake all night with its groaning and creaking. For some reason, the tree continued to shelter him, despite the storm that Benitoyo felt swirling around him.

In the morning, Benitoyo felt as though the tree had aged overnight. The trunk appeared more gray than brown or green. Its leaves were no longer shiny, but had a dull gray hue to them.

Feeling foolish, Benitoyo reached into his bag and pulled out a tiny uncut emerald, just a sliver, really. He still took a moment, bowing his head in thanks, then pushing the gem beneath the soil at the root of the tree.

"Thank you again for your excellent hospitality," he said. He reached out and patted the hard bark.

Had it just been his imagination that the tree had actually sheltered him? He realized that for the first time in many nights he hadn't had a nightmare.

But he couldn't stay here. He had to get back home.

Benitoyo crossed out of fields midday and started down the road, heading toward Yawatan. Though he didn't have the greatest landsense, he still knew the general direction of his home.

Nothing bad happened that night. Benitoyo found a farmer's barn to sleep in, and the farmer sold him some soft cheese and bread, as well as refilling his water flagons.

The days soon took on a familiar pattern: waking and eating a small amount of whatever he'd managed to scrounge the day before. Walking all morning, his landsense directing him due west. Taking a longish break during the middle of the day, finding some sort of shade away from the awful corpse flowers and spiky grasses. Then walking until dusk.

Benitoyo saw very few people on the road, either going toward Jinyi or toward Yawatan. Most people were staying at home, afraid of how the land had changed. Farmers complained about their crops rotting in the fields. Strange birds now flew overhead, with large leathery wings like bats, who would tear apart the rotting food, scattering the seeds before the farmer could glean the fields.

He knew that the border was getting close. He could feel it in the way the land seemed to flow better under his feet. It was as if it was getting easier to walk.

Soon, he would be in his homelands. And though he told himself that he'd go back to Jinyi, particularly if Shimokoro or Darikuto ordered it, he knew that he'd never return voluntarily.

The corpse flowers had multiplied on this stretch of road. Benitoyo found himself wearing a mask to stop at least some of the stench. The sun beat down hard on his covered head. He was going to run out of water soon. Hopefully he'd find a farmer willing to share his well once he crossed the border.

It wouldn't do to stretch his body out on the ground around here. Beyond the flowers and the spiked grass was rot and stinking marshlands. Bugs buzzed around his head, gnats that whined and set his teeth on edge.

It had never been like this before, in all the times he'd crossed between the lands.

Foothills rose up before him. The cool green soothed his watering eyes. Just a little while longer, and he'd be home.

"Hey there," came a voice out of nowhere.

Benitoyo startled and stumbled, nearly falling over before he caught himself.

Someone had been standing next to the road. Had Benitoyo just not seen him? Or had he mistaken the man standing before him as a boulder?

The man had the dark, reddish hued skin of Kinaki and some of the warriors. But the grin he gave was easy going, almost putting Benitoyo at ease. He wore traveling clothes— a dark gray shirt and brown pants that had both seen better days. His hat was straw, so weathered it looked brown instead of yellowish. A heavy-looking rucksack was attached to his back, and he carried a solid walking stick as well.

Benitoyo shook his head at himself. Really, he just hadn't been paying attention. The man hadn't appeared out of nowhere.

"Good day to you," Benitoyo said before he resolutely started walking again.

"Say, don't I know you?" the other man said, falling easily into step with Benitoyo.

Benitoyo glanced over at the other man. Did he look familiar? There was something about his eyes…

"No," Benitoyo said, resolutely looking forward. He just had to get across the border. He didn't understand why that need was suddenly so strong. He'd start running, if he could, if it wouldn't have been so impolite.

"I'm sure I know you from somewhere. You live in Jinyi, right? At the palace?"

"I do some business there," Benitoyo said stiffly. His sense of unease grew. There was something not right with this man, this traveler, walking easily beside him.

"Aww, don't be modest," the other man said. "You've done a lot of business there. Particularly with Kinaki, and the fine powder you put into his salt over the years."

Benitoyo's mouth suddenly went dry. "I have no idea what you're talking about," he said sternly.

"Of course you don't," the man said, his tone mocking. "You were just following orders. Passing along information. You didn't do anything wrong."

Benitoyo shivered but kept walking. The day had suddenly gotten so much colder. He should have welcomed the breeze, but it blew at him from a cold place.

"Now, I just want to give you a little reward, for all that you've done," the man said. He almost sounded sincere, as if he really did have something good for Benitoyo. "It isn't much. Just a sliver, deep in your soul."

"What do you mean?" Benitoyo asked. His nightmares of Sunli swallowing him whole came back in full force.

"Just a little extra to carry home with you. To spread around there. You wouldn't want to leave everything behind here in the House of Cobalt, would you? No, you should take part of these lands back with you," the man said.

Benitoyo pressed his lips together and shook his head. No. He didn't want to bring anything from these lands home with him.

"Hold out your hand," the man said.

Horrified, Benitoyo found his hand reaching out. He tried to stop himself, but there was some magic at work here that he didn't understand.

Or was he still dreaming? Still under that great oak who had sheltered him so many nights before?

The man slipped a sliver of wood into Benitoyo's palm. It was as thin as a seamstress's fine pin, and no longer than the first knuckle of his forefinger. It disappeared under his skin, leaving only a faint red mark behind.

And a fire that burned, deep inside his body, as though his blood had suddenly grown fevered.

"Go now. Spread your seed far and wide!" the man said, falling behind as Benitoyo hurried on.

A rock in the road tripped Benitoyo. He staggered and fell, striking his head.

When Benitoyo woke, he found himself sitting on the side of the road, resting against a convenient boulder. The border between the lands was close, so close. An hour or less, and he'd be there.

Had he dreamed of his encounter with the mysterious man? That would make the most sense. Though why would he stop just short of the border?

Although—Benitoyo always took a midday nap. And the sun was well past its zenith, now, when it had been directly overhead before.

There was a slightly tender, red spot in the middle of his right palm. Maybe when he sat down he bruised it on a rock.

No matter.

There was nothing wrong with him. It had all been a dream. Soon, he'd be home. And he'd never leave again.

To that, he'd swear.

Chapter Twenty-Nine

HOUSE OF CRYSTAL

AKALINA COULD HAVE SWORN that mist started creeping into the sitting room where she, the Holder Sitre, and a few others had gathered. Though Akalina wasn't the LandHolder, she was still considered to be part of the LandHolder's household. At more than one Hold along her journey, she'd spent the evening listening to grievances and giving advice.

It was a strange world, where adults like the Holders might turn to her for counsel.

The room was cold, like every place else in the Hold, despite the large hearth and heated stones. That Holder Sitre still was able to perform routine magic was impressive. The chairs were mismatched and nothing was new. Flat gray slate made up the floor and showed the paths that people had worn walking across it.

Windows opposite the hearth looked out onto a dark garden. That was where Akalina saw the mist. Like white fog, it gathered and swirled on the ground first, then inched up.

It took Akalina a few moments to realize it wasn't actually fog or mist.

All the ghosts had gathered together and were slowly coalescing into their usual form.

Akalina had never seen that many ghosts massed together. Not even during ghost month.

She turned her attention to the Holder, only now realizing that the woman had fallen still.

A smile of satisfaction and peace filled Sitre's face.

"The LandHolder has come," she said simply.

Akalina blinked, startled. She'd thought that she would have felt when Yimifut took on the mantel of the land. She stretched out her landsense but honestly, she didn't feel that much difference.

The ghosts obviously did, however. While a few stood in the corners of the room, most had amassed outside. They filled the entire garden with their unearthly glow.

Akalina hoped that their cold wouldn't hurt the flowers growing there.

She took a moment and looked at the others sitting in the room. They all appeared to be marveling at their luck that a LandHolder had been chosen. No one seemed angry that Yimifut had taken his time, refusing the land at first.

Suddenly, Yimifut appeared in the middle of the room. Akalina blinked, surprised. She'd never seen such magic before, not in all her time with Ibitsima.

"There is another LandHolder here," he growled, addressing the room. Then he turned to stare at Akalina.

She could see the differences in him, how becoming the LandHolder had already changed him. His hair had grown longer and bushed out, the black curls circling his face like a living crown. The gray of his eyes had paled, washed out like old clouds. His clothes had grown darker.

"We will need to oust this usurper," Yimifut said. His eyes bore into her, his stare heavy and hot. "We will need to do whatever it takes to defeat him."

"We?" Akalina said. She didn't know why she wasn't surprised that he wanted her to join this battle.

"Yes. You. And all the ghosts you can muster," he said.

All the ghosts? Why would he want ghosts? They couldn't affect the living, not normally.

He turned to Sitre. "Holder. I need your warriors."

"They are yours," Sitre said. She seemed bemused by his request. "Keep us safe, LandHolder."

Had she known that her son had become the LandHolder? The others in the room seemed quite surprised.

Akalina felt a pang of sorrow that she'd never know what it was like to have that sort of knowledge or relationship, between a mother and son.

Then Yimifut gathered her up. Without taking a single step, she was suddenly elsewhere.

Her landsense told her that she was west of the capital, almost in the center of the lands of the House of Crystal.

Just like that.

In front of her, a large pavilion had been raised. It was big enough to shelter thirty people from the rain. Magic swirled around it. She could see it, a haze like her ghosts, only with purple and golden hues in it.

She suddenly remembered a poem she'd heard about the Chamber of Crystals, the golden light that spilled out from within. This magic had that same feel to it.

An army was spread out on all sides of the pavilion, surrounding it.

They were also surrounding Akalina, Yimifut, and the few warriors he'd brought from the Hold.

"Stop!" Yimifut commanded.

Akalina was impressed by how he sounded, so firm and in control. Not like a fifteen-year-old boy who'd just upended his entire world.

The magic swirling around the pavilion dropped down. It

didn't disappear, but lay like a morass of power rolling along the ground. Akalina found herself fascinated by the eddies and swirls in it, as if the magic had formed itself into a thick, viscous river.

"No," came the response from inside the tent. "You cannot stop me."

It took Akalina a moment to recognize Darikuto's voice. It had turned more melodic since the last time she'd heard it. But he also sounded drunk. Maybe drunk with power?

"Yes, I can," Yimifut said. He strode forward. The warriors he'd brought with him circled around their LandHolder, all facing outward, as if they thought they could protect him from being overwhelmed by the army around them.

Akalina stayed where she was, alone, forgotten.

She tried to make herself seem meek and small. There was no good reason for her to be here. Nothing she could do. Except possibly to witness the slaughter of her LandHolder.

Darikuto laughed. It wasn't a warm, friendly sound. Instead, it sent further chills down Akalina's spine.

It was only then that she realized that the ghosts had all come with her. Plus, more had arrived, flowing into the area where the army was camped.

Despite the cold, Akalina's heart suddenly warmed.

The LandHolder wasn't alone. There was a reason he'd brought her. She and all the ghosts weren't just witnesses.

No, he'd brought her because the power flowing around the pavilion, the heart of the House of Crystal, could not only be used by the two LandHolders.

But by the ghosts as well.

Usually, ghosts couldn't affect the living. Not normally.

Not unless they sacrificed themselves. Died again.

Forever this time.

Whatever it takes.

Akalina nodded grimly.

Yimifut must have foreseen this battle. He'd also told her that he had only been able to see a short way into the future after he made his choice.

Would they win this battle?

They had to.

Whatever it takes.

Chapter Thirty

HOUSE OF COBALT

Gray dawn greeted Chaotu as he opened his eyes in an unfamiliar tent, on a stranger's cot, in borrowed clothes.

Maybe it was fall already, and the winter rains had returned. Maybe the nightmare was over. Maybe the world was returning to normal.

The sun broke through the clouds on the horizon just a few moments later. Light and heat returned to the world, heralding the continuation of his nightmares.

He wouldn't bother eating that morning—though the ritual didn't call for it, he wanted to be in a fasted, cleansed state.

That way, if the nauseous feeling he had just thinking about the ceremony took a physical form, there wouldn't be anything in his stomach to vomit up.

He put on more borrowed clothes: a long robe made of a green so pale it almost appeared white. It had been modified greatly for his shorter stature. They'd left the cuffs on the sleeves wide and huge, though. He had to take care every time he moved his arms or he'd knock something over.

When the guards pulled back the flap of the tent he was staying in, he nodded at them. He was ready.

Chaotu had no idea if he'd survive the coming ritual. There was a chance that after he renounced his heritage that the lands of the House of Gold might accept him and he would regain both his magic as well as his landsense.

There was also a chance that he'd live forever broken, with nowhere to call home.

It was worth the risk. Anything to oust that damned demon who'd swallowed the soul of the LandHolder.

Even in his thoughts, Chaotu couldn't call him Father. That was too painful.

No, better to think that his father had died, long ago, and an imposter now claimed the title of LandHolder.

Chaotu followed the guards up to the top of a hill, ready to demonstrate his intent to stay in the lands of the House of Gold. He was going to go through the ritual in front of the armies. Then, if he survived, he'd lead a Vein of warriors into battle.

Borrowed armies as well.

Unnir had agreed to allow them to hedge their bets. Only Chaotu would renounce his heritage. Lijun would not, at least not yet. That way, there was a chance that the lands of the House of Cobalt might return to her.

It was a slim chance. Most of the legends behind such matters were clear that once a potential heir had made their home elsewhere, the Land would never choose them.

But these times were unlike any that had come before.

Chaotu didn't want to give up his heritage, his lands, his beloved home.

However, he hated the thing that had become the LandHolder more. It would be enough to ease his pain if he faced the LandHolder again under the aegis of a different House. Then killed him.

All the priests and priestesses of the various temples stood behind Chaotu. Only Torja stood beside him. Her gray eyes looked haunted. She was gaunt as a farmer who'd lost all his crops. The sharpness of her features didn't match the warmth of her smile.

"I would have loved to have foreseen this," she whispered at him with a broad wink.

Chaotu tried not to frown at her levity. This was a serious matter.

With a sigh, Torja's expression grew dark and foreboding. "You understand the consequences of your actions? This ritual bears serious costs. Once we have started, you cannot change your mind."

"I understand," Chaotu said. He stood up taller, and spoke clearly, letting his words ring out, so that all who witnessed this could hear.

"I hereby renounce my heritage, all allegiance to the House of Cobalt. I will never take a free breath there again. I freely give up any claim I may have to that land. I will never willingly return to that land."

It had to just be Chaotu's imagination that the sun was suddenly slightly dimmer.

"So you have said, so let it be known," Torja said. Her words echoed out as well.

Were some happy at his choice? Pleased that the House of Cobalt had fallen so far?

Chaotu shivered as Torja raised her hands, magic rising with the gesture. Chaotu shivered again as it descended on him, like cool rain.

"Don't fight it," Torja whispered as she pushed more magic down onto him.

Chaotu drew in on himself. He'd only read of people being banished before. No one had ever written about what it felt like.

At first, it wasn't so bad. He felt like a hillside covered with loose dirt that the rain was washing away. He wouldn't allow himself to pant once he started to feel, well, *less* than what he had been.

Then the rain grew harsher, Torrents formed above and around him, the rain slashing down, each drop like a burning pellet.

He blinked, looking out, surprised to see sunlight surrounding him.

The rain formed claws, raking down his sides, tearing into his flesh, seeking that thing that had made him whole. He cried out. He couldn't help it.

He took some satisfaction at how hard Torja flinched at the sound.

But she was merciless. His puny cries would not make her falter. Her eyes were like black storm clouds, sucking at his soul.

Down came the rain. All his senses were drown in the torrent of magic around him. It tore away his landsense and dissolved his connection to his house.

Still the raindrops struck him, burrowing deep under his skin until all he knew was water and pain. Every inch of him was on fire despite the cold quenching rain, his bones grinding together as he shook.

A loud clap of thunder boomed out as Chaotu felt the last of him get washed away.

He'd started as a solid hill of dirt. He ended as a thin toothpick, naked and shivering. He was weak as a sapling, transplanted in foreign soil.

Could he thrive here?

He looked around him with blind eyes. Sure, he could see. But for the first time, he had no idea which way was south, the former land of his heart. He would have to check the sun to determine which direction was east or west.

He was bereft, at sea on solid ground.

"Rest, now," Torja told him quietly. "Be patient. Give it some time. Give yourself a chance to heal."

Chaotu shook his head at her. No, he had more to do. The LandHolder, *his* LandHolder, Unnir, had yet another task for him.

Landless, he still forged on, watching his feet at first to make sure he didn't trip, as he could only feel the ground physically. It wasn't rising up to meet him.

Soon, he would borrow some armor. And an army.

Then go and face his former LandHolder. Make sure Kinaki realized that not only was his son still alive, but that he'd renounced the House of Cobalt forever.

Chapter Thirty-One
HOUSE OF GOLD

EMIL WASN'T certain that Unnir's plan made sense. I mean, sure, it tickled his black heart to rub it in Kinaki's face, that his only son had turned on him. Particularly after the last week and some of the stunning losses that the House of Gold had suffered.

However, Chaotu wasn't a warrior. Not really. He was much more like Vide in temperament. He should probably be behind the lines working strategy, not out in front, commanding a Vein of men.

His sister, though, was no better suited for the duty. Plus, Kinaki, like Yudur, had favored his boy above his girl. Lijun turning against him wouldn't bother Kinaki as much.

Wouldn't Yudur be surprised now? Emil taking Unnir's commands, even Vide listening to her? She'd become a much better LandHolder than Emil had ever considered possible.

Not that he'd ever tell her that. Or Vide.

But after the war, Emil was looking forward to having his own Hold, away from Haravik. Just him and Vide. Though at some point Emil would marry, and would raise a passel of kids.

Something, anything, to remind him of life after all the death he'd seen.

For now, he stood on the battlefield with two of the other VeinHolders, watching Chaotu's performance.

The boy was desperate to confront his father. Emil had sympathy for that. There was more than once that he'd wanted to raise Yudur's ghost and yell at him for the choices he'd made while he'd been alive.

Choices that had included shunting Unnir to the side. The House of Gold wouldn't have had so many issues at the start of her rule if she'd been better trained.

Not that he and Vide had made it any easier.

"He's in trouble again," Gudli said sourly. "The demons are fighting better today."

Emil nodded. It was as if the demons had finally started listening to their human counterparts, and had figured out that there was more to battle than just surging forward in a line and attacking.

They were forming pockets now, luring in the warriors from the House of Gold, then closing them off, isolating them. Emil had fought his way through to free warriors that way. And been yelled at for risking himself.

He couldn't help it. No one should die alone, not on a battlefield.

"I'll dig him out this time," Emil said, placing his peaked helmet on his head, tightening the leather strap under his neck.

Chaotu had already announced his presence on the battlefield. Leading a group of warriors from the House of Gold had spurred on the other army, making them fight harder. Dirtier.

Which had been the fear all along. That instead of demoralizing the opposing army, Chaotu's defection would energize them.

Emil drew hard on his magic as he strode into the fray, two dozen warriors at his sides. He could call for more if he needed. Hopefully, he was only risking this group.

No matter the amount of cleansing winds that Emil drew up, the battlefield stunk. It wasn't the stench of the gore, or even the sweat and fear of the living that bothered him as much as the ashy scent carried by the demons. That constant smell of smoke reminded him that nothing really lived any longer in the lands of the House of Cobalt. Everything was corrupted there, even the earth itself.

His job was to win the war. Drive Kinaki back. Ensure that his losses were so great that he would have to withdraw.

They couldn't give an inch on their border. Or all the lands of the House of Gold would be lost as well.

Emil used his great sword with both hands to clear a path through the fighters to get to Chaotu. He used what magic he could to push away his foes, not relying on physical strength alone. He would need to refresh himself afterward, but they'd counted on that.

Chaotu was still valiantly fighting, as far as Emil could tell. He knew how to defend himself. But he couldn't lead. He just waded in and fought. Almost like a demon, though everyone from Unnir and Torja down to Vide had verified that Chaotu was of the living. He bore not demon.

"You're going to be surrounded!" Emil shouted, willing his words to be carried to Chaotu's ears.

The boy had no landsense, as they'd seen earlier. He got turned around on the battlefield, confused by the noise and chaos. He had a good warrior beside him, though, who would point him in the right direction.

Chaotu grimly fought on in the same direction he'd been going, possibly unable to hear Emil's words, as most of his magic was gone as well.

With a sigh, Emil directed his warriors to opening up the

trap about to fall shut around Chaotu. Damn it! They shouldn't have sent him into battle. Not yet.

And that was the other thing that bothered Emil so much about the war. Not the loss of life so much as the loss of potential.

Like a field being harvested before the wheat had sprouted. Such a waste.

Finally, Emil drew beside Chaotu, close enough for him to hear. "You need to follow me!"

Chaotu's eyes grew big. He looked like a boy, playing in armor that was too large for him.

Except for the blood on his sword, the dirt and gore spattered across his shield.

"You!" Emil shouted at the warrior who had been guiding Chaotu. "Take us back to the ridge!"

The older man grunted and nodded grimly. He turned immediately and started back, slaying the demon who thought this was a good opportunity to rush forward.

"Follow him! I'll be behind you!" Emil said.

Fortunately, Chaotu didn't fight Emil and instead, fell into step behind the older warrior. The pair of them would make it.

Emil didn't see the demon who threw the ax into his back. It penetrated his armor instead of bouncing off it, as most of the weapons did.

He gasped and the world grew cold. Without meaning to, Emil dropped to his knees.

Ugh. The dirt around here was so disgusting. Vide would be yelling at him for days about it.

Emil called upon what magic he could to lift himself back up to his feet.

But he had crossed the border. He knelt in the lands of the House of Cobalt. There was no true land here for him to call upon, no clean magic he could use.

It felt like sucking ashes deep into his lungs, choking him so he couldn't breathe.

None of the others saw him fall. That was all right. He wouldn't have wanted them to risk themselves for a dead man.

There was no second blow. None was needed. His life bled out quickly, swallowed by greedy land. He lay on the cold, ashy ground, his head to the side, and wondered whether Vide would follow him to the underworld, just so he could yell at his brother for dying too soon.

Before the end of the war.

Then the world faded, and all the questions and the pain drained away.

Chapter Thirty-Two

HOUSE OF PEARL

DARIKUTO FELT it when that usurper claimed the mantle of the lands of the House of Crystal. It was as though he'd been covered in a warm blanket of power, only to have it slowly be drawn away from him, first exposing his shoulders, then his torso, and further on down.

Pulling as much of the magic from his own land as he could channel, Darikuto snatched back at the blanket, that cape of power, trying to draw it back over himself.

It wasn't much of a fight. The land easily pulled away, settling itself on another.

Darikuto blinked. The army was still spread out before him, beyond the pavilion, a dark mass ready to rend and tear any opponent to bits. Behind him stood the priests from the various temples, bathing in the light under the pavilion. Sweet incense from the ritual still wreathed him, and the air was cool against his flushed skin.

Another spike of power coursed through him. He shook his head, trying to clear his senses.

He was still connected to this land he realized. The other hadn't claimed it soon enough.

Just past the pavilion a fog of mist arose. Untapped magic that hadn't settled on either claimant yet.

A boy stood there, with a paltry few warriors around him. Country bumpkins who didn't have the training or skill of the least of Chuyoko's people. He was tall enough, Darikuto supposed, though he hadn't come into his full height yet. Wild black curls surrounded his face, like a puffed up chick trying to fend off a predator. His eyes were nearly colorless, blazing white with power.

"Stop!" the boy demanded.

Darikuto couldn't help but reply, "No. You cannot stop me." He felt invincible. This upstart would soon learn the true meaning of power.

"Yes, I can," the boy said. Strange, he sounded so much older than he looked.

But Darikuto was having none of it. He laughed in the boy's face, at his puny threats.

Then Darikuto reached out and tapped into the rolling mass of power that stood between them, the unclaimed magic that few could wield. He blasted the boy (he refused to give him his proper title of LandHolder).

Just like that, the boy flew backwards, out of the circle and into the night.

However, he didn't tumble down, into the mass of waiting men. He went up into the air, like a damned bird, hovering there against the sky, his terrible eyes shining like twin pieces of the moon.

He reached out with both hands and made a pulling motion, as if he'd also thought about the land as a blanket, and was pulling it back toward him, away from Darikuto.

Too bad the boy just didn't have the years of wisdom and accumulated land knowledge that Darikuto had. Or he would have attacked Darikuto directly.

He would have failed, of course. But focusing on the land was just as much of a failure.

Darikuto laughed again and spun up some of the waiting magic, throwing it at the boy again. He made such a good target, hovering there with his glowing eyes.

This time, the boy spun around, as if caught in a terrible tornado.

Darikuto used the time while the boy wasn't attacking to draw more magic into himself.

Wait. There was considerably less magic than there had been just a few moments ago.

What was sucking up all that power?

Darikuto glanced around. He finally noticed that a young woman stood there, with black hair and pale features. A few of the boy's warriors stood guard around her, though no one was threatening her.

Why hadn't she been grabbed? Chuyoko's people were falling down in their jobs. Those few paltry warriors that Yimifut had brought with him surely weren't strong enough to actually protect her.

Much of the white mist of power had gathered around her. Strange. She shouldn't be able to direct it, not like a LandHolder.

Then he heard the first of his own warriors scream in terror.

That wasn't mist.

Those were *ghosts*.

She was at the heart of them, directing them against his warriors.

How did a ghost have enough power to affect the living?

They were the ones sucking up all that power. It was not going to go back into the land. The lands of the House of Crystal were going to be weaker as a result.

Before Darikuto could return his attention to what was in front of him, the boy attacked.

Vines around Darikuto's feet sprang up, holding him in place. Knife-sharp winds buffeted him from side to side, slicing open his cheek, bruising his chest, battering at his arms and legs.

Darikuto tried to fight back. He drew up power from his own lands, and instantly recognized his mistake.

The vines holding him bled off much of that power, greedily sucking it away and draining it back into the land surrounding him.

Which ultimately would power the LandHolder opposing him.

Darikuto still fought off the attack as best he could. He surrounded himself with a shield of power, cutting off the winds. With a power blast, he disintegrated the vines holding him. Then he formed a blade of pure flame and flew out of the pavilion, ready to meet the boy on a field of battle.

He was, after all, just a boy. He knew nothing of being a warrior.

A pillar of ghostly white followed after him, like a blind snake seeking its prey.

He heard the sound of battle beneath him, as his warriors tried to fight the shadows that attacked them.

He just had to get the boy to back down. Just a little. So that Darikuto could wrest the land away from him.

The boy seemed to have other ideas.

He had the temerity to laugh, to *laugh*, at Darikuto.

"You won't find this funny once you feel the sharp edge of my sword, boy," Darikuto roared.

"Oh, I'm certain of that," the boy said. "My name is Yimifut. I am the LandHolder for the House of Crystal. You have the rest of the night to pack up and leave my lands."

"No," Darikuto said. "You will fight me and the winner shall take all."

Yimifut laughed again. "Why should I do that? Your army is being decimated. Your own powers grow weaker. You are nothing but a greedy bully, preying on those you falsely believe to not be as strong as you."

Darikuto felt the truth of those words strike him harder than any polearm. "You cannot kill me," he said. When had he started panting?

He looked down, only to see that the long chain of ghosts had found him, and were snuggly wrapped around his ankles. He could flee them, but only if he left the lands of the House of Crystal.

"Why not?" Yimifut asked seriously. "None of the other LandHolders would find fault with my decision. It is completely within my rights."

"You cannot take the lands of the House of Pearl. You are too young, too inexperienced," Darikuto said. He tried to put as much scorn into his tone as possible. "And all of us have a greater threat to face. The House of Cobalt."

For just a moment, those piercing white eyes shifted away from Darikuto and looked toward the south, as if he could see the truth of what was happening down there, how Unnir battled for her life against a demon army.

And was losing.

Yimifut focused back on Darikuto before he could try anything. Waves of power wrapped around him, tighter than any ropes.

"In exchange for your life, you will offer all your armies to Unnir, to fight off that thing that Kinaki has become," Yimifut commanded.

The blankets of magic surrounding Darikuto squeezed tighter. Just once. Just enough to let him know that despite what he might want to believe, he really was in danger. It would take a lot of power, possibly more than Darikuto could muster, in order to break free.

This boy, this Yimifut, would kill him.

And possibly laugh all the while.

"I accept your terms," Darikuto said. "Here are some of mine. You, too, must muster an army to go help Unnir. We will have a truce until such time as Kinaki is defeated."

Darikuto could tell that Yimifut didn't like those terms. He wanted to disagree. He'd just come into his power, just taken on the mantle of his Land. To leave now would be very difficult for him to do.

It would make him weaker in the long run. Though his land had already been weakened by the ghosts, draining off the easy power Darikuto had raised.

He was going to have to find out who that young woman was, where she had come from. How did she have such control over the ghosts?

She was going to have to become part of The New Plan.

"Fine," Yimifut said after a few moments. "I will gather together the warriors of the House of Crystal and throw them at Kinaki's army. But we will all be too late."

He abruptly released Darikuto, catching him off guard. Darikuto dropped down precipitously fast before he straightened himself out.

"Leave by the dawn," Yimifut warned again.

Then he disappeared, taking his warriors, the ghosts, and the young woman with him.

Darikuto slowly descended to the earth. It felt cold to him, now. Unfriendly. No longer welcoming. Filled with sharp crystals and waiting snow.

The priests and warriors all looked to him when he arrived.

"Break camp. Be ready to leave before dawn," he announced.

"We could have taken them," Chuyoko growled at him.

She looked so much paler than he'd ever seen her. What had fighting with the ghosts done to her? What had it cost her and the others?

"We leave before dawn," Darikuto repeated. "Use all the magic you need to."

Then he strode out of the pavilion, out of the lighted space, dissolving into the darkness.

The land was not the only thing that felt different. He, too, had been changed.

He could sense that deep, *deep* level of bedrock that connected all the lands together now. Not just the House of Pearl and the House of Crystal. No, it lay under the House of Gold as well as the House of Cobalt. Stretched all the way down into the barbarian lands, though it petered out after a short while there, butted up against a second plate of land.

The mountains to the north were not part of that vital essence. No, they came from a different place, shoved up into being when the two bedrocks had collided.

Darikuto understood much more, now, about the true nature of power.

He would need to meditate on how to incorporate all that knowledge into The New Plan.

Chapter Thirty-Three

HOUSE OF CRYSTAL

MENHAPTU SAT IN HIS STUDY, comfortably sipping a glass of wine.

The LandHolder had returned.

A sense of tension that Menhaptu hadn't realized he'd been holding on to had gradually drained away. He felt as though he could finally take a deep breath. He could light stones again, and didn't need those pesky candles. Windows that overlooked the back garden could be open, without fear of being inundated with gnats or eaten alive by mosquitoes.

Menhaptu reveled in how *normal* everything felt.

He wasn't surprised that whoever had become the new LandHolder hadn't yet shown up in Nyati. They were probably driving off Darikuto, sending him packing.

And good riddance.

Menhaptu could hardly wait until he met the new LandHolder. He had his report all prepared, how he would subtly oust all the older priests and priestesses who had put Menhaptu in charge, just so they could continue to run things in the background, without putting their own skin at risk.

Revenge was going to be so sweet.

The LandHolder would clean house in all the temples, Menhaptu was certain. It hadn't been just the Temple of Truth who'd lost their leader.

Such a shame. Such a waste.

Maybe the LandHolder would decide to do something about that as well, to avenge Ibitsima's death. But first, surely the LandHolder would see to the Chamber of Crystals, and remove the rot that had set in there.

Menhaptu took another sip of really, such an excellent white wine. Subtly smoky, with hints of pear and apple. Delicious.

Suddenly, a boy, no, a young man, stood in front of Menhaptu.

The only one who would have that sort of power would be the new LandHolder.

"Greetings, LandHolder!" Menhaptu said, standing. "I am Menhaptu, head of the Temple of Truth."

"I know," the young man said. "I am Yimifut."

Only then did Menhaptu realize that someone stood beside Yimifut. It took him a moment to place the girl. Ah. Akalina.

He shifted from one foot to the other, uneasy. She was the one who'd started all this trouble.

"I need you to gather your people, and be ready to go in the morning," Yimifut said.

"Go? Go where?" Menhaptu said. The same feeling of unease, when the land had been unsettled, came rushing back.

"Unnir needs our help. She won't be able to survive the war with Kinaki for much longer," Yimifut said grimly.

It sounded as though he was pronouncing a doom on all their heads.

And he was, in a way.

"LandHolder, as you sure that's wise?" Menhaptu said. "You shouldn't be leaving your land so soon after you've acquired it!"

More than one story was told about wandering LandHolders, who didn't fully cement their relationship with the land before traveling to another's. It left their own land, as well as their people, weaker.

Menhaptu feared that if Yimifut left now, parts of the lands of the House of Crystal would remain wild.

"I am aware of the consequences," Yimifut said. "What happens if I leave, as well as what happens if I stay."

Menhaptu blinked. He hadn't realized that the situation to the south was so dire.

"Are you certain?" Menhaptu had to check. After all, Yimifut appeared to be a younger man. Maybe he hadn't thought everything all the way through, and would benefit from the wisdom of his elders.

Yimifut turned his head, looking at Akalina. He gave her a small, sad smile.

It wasn't the smile of a young man for his beloved. No, it looked more like someone sharing pain with another.

"Maybe that will become the motto of my Hold," he said. "*Whatever it takes.*"

Akalina nodded. She looked even more serious than the last time Menhaptu had seen her. Her skin was so pale, as if she'd become part ghost.

Maybe she had. Her eyes looked black and unfathomable when she turned them to Menhaptu.

"Whatever it takes," she repeated. "Even if it's the loss of magic for the House of Crystal. Even if it's the loss of all the ghosts. It might be the only way any of the lands survive."

Menhaptu's throat was suddenly dry. He unconsciously reached for his glass of wine and took a great gulp.

These...these...*children* were going to strip the House of Crystal of all that it had. In an effort to do what?

"Gather your things and people," Yimifut said again. "We will leave at dawn. You will be coming with us whether you're ready or not."

Then Yimifut and Akalina vanished, leaving Menhaptu alone in his study. The night was suddenly much colder than it had been.

Menhaptu downed the rest of his wine, letting its warmth sear his throat, willing it to descend all the way into his belly.

Surely what they were going to face couldn't be that bad.

Could it?

Chapter Thirty-Four
HOUSE OF COBALT

KINAKI ROARED WITH DISPLEASURE. He strode behind the mass of the army, fighting desperately against the House of Gold warriors.

His son was alive. *Alive!* That meant Lijun was probably alive as well.

Even though Kinaki might have sent warriors to put an end to his son's rebellion, he had still been saddened by the loss. As well as the necessity.

For Chaotu to show up with an army of the House of Gold at his back? Stinking of them? Having renounced his heritage?

It wasn't to be tolerated.

How dare he? *How dare he?*

Kinaki roared again, a mighty howl that gave his warriors more strength, more courage, against the mightier foe.

But they wouldn't be outnumbered for long.

Kinaki turned to Wanho. He knew that the CollierHolders would think it odd, Kinaki talking to himself.

The WarHolders knew the truth.

"I need to bring the other armies in," he said. "Now."

Kinaki felt Wanho adjust his grip around their shared body.

Yesss. But there isss a cosssst. The Time of Great Pain is Here.

Kinaki paused for a moment. Wanho had mentioned the Time of Great Pain before. The demon couldn't be more articulate than that. Just that decisions and choices would need to be made.

Fine. Kinaki would make them.

"I don't care what the cost is," Kinaki ground out. "I need them here. Now."

While as LandHolder, Kinaki had the power to move large groups of people with him, it was a different thing to pick up a group who were far away and bring them to where he was.

Wanho shifted again.

You will come with me, to the underworld. There, we will reach the warriors. And carry them through overnight. They will be on this side in the morning.

Kinaki gulped. He feared going to the underworld. He didn't want to see what it was actually like there. Wanho would protect him, of course. He needed Kinaki, just as Kinaki needed the demon.

But still.

"Whatever it takes," he said grimly, feeling the words echo out as if he'd just pronounced an augury.

Or a doom.

Darkness surrounded him and he felt his soul slide down, below the cool earth, even farther than the deepest of his mines.

Down and down, into the earth.

When he stopped, he had to blink to clear his eyes.

A snake rested on a grand throne before him. The serpent's eyes were the brilliant blue of pure cobalt. Red, white, and black patterns made up its scales.

Kinaki suddenly realized that he was naked, just bare red-brown skin. He had no sword, no armor. Cold mud squished between his toes. His belly hung over his waist, and his arms were flabby. He had no strength left in his body at all.

Wanho had left him weak. Without the demon's magic wrapped around him, Kinaki had no power.

The snake reared up on its throne.

No, not merely a snake.

Wanho.

The demon dislodged its jaw, opening its mouth wide, as if to swallow Kinaki whole.

For a moment, Kinaki stood trembling before the demon.

But they weren't completely on a magical plane, in the underworld.

Kinaki could still feel the Land surrounding him.

Not only that, but he was far enough down that he could reach for the bedrock, the plates that connected all the lands. The reason why he could be the sole LandHolder someday.

He dug his toes into the good earth and called on his power, ready to fight the demon for his continued breath.

After this stupid contest of wills, Kinaki would fetch his armies and throw them at Unnir's puny forces.

He would rule them all.

Chapter Thirty-Five

HOUSE OF GOLD

UNNIR SLEPT POORLY. She dreamed her land was unsettled. She would reach for something simple, like a piece of wood, and it would shy away, out of her hand. It was only when she put serious effort into focusing on her magic that she could get anything done.

However, when Unnir awoke, she felt a greater sense of calm than she'd known before going to sleep. She laid on her cot and reached out with her landsense, trying to determine what was different.

Ahhhh. The lands of the House of Crystal had found their LandHolder. All along that border, both lands were now calm.

Good. Maybe now they could send her some help. She wouldn't ask for help from Darikuto. He'd been the one who'd killed Ibitsima. His grand plans had put all the houses at risk.

Grief descended on Unnir as she lay there, making her tired limbs feel heavier. Emil had been killed the day before. She'd had to order warriors to hold onto Vide before he destroyed half the camp when he'd learned the news.

Hopefully he would be able to see reason now, though she doubted that he'd be of any use for quite some time.

The brothers had always been ridiculously close. It had peeved her as a young girl, never being included in anything.

Now, though she'd never been close to Emil, she still felt his death keenly. He'd turned into a good leader, a good VeinHolder. He would have been a much better person after the war, she felt certain.

Kinaki had more to answer for.

Slowly, Unnir made herself rise from her cot. She dressed in plain robes, much plainer than what she used to wear. She just couldn't be bothered with the formality that the rest of the court held so dearly.

Not here. Not now.

A messenger stood waiting for her, in the open area just past the curtain that separated off her cot.

"What is it?" Unnir asked, fear stabbing at her heart. Had Vide taken his own life the night before?

"You need to see this," the messenger stated grimly.

Unnir nodded and followed the messenger out of her tent. Warriors milled around restlessly. Everyone was muttering. An undercurrent of fear tugged at her, turning the sweet morning air bitter.

The messenger wove through the crowds and up onto the hillside that was closest. Then she pointed at the distance.

Unnir recoiled in horror.

On the far side of the border, just west of Kinaki's main camp, a dark hole had opened. It looked like a small volcano had taken off the top of the nearby hill.

Warriors were spilling out of the hole. Hundreds of them. They ran down the hill to join with the rest of Kinaki's army.

Unnir looked out over the rest of Kinaki's warriors. They'd doubled in number, easily.

"Send—send more messengers. To the new LandHolder in the House of Gold. And to Darikuto. Tell them...tell them we are at our darkest hour. If they don't send help now, there will be no one left to send help to," Unnir commanded.

The messenger whirled away, fear adding speed to her steps.

Unnir watched for a moment as the hill continued to vomit up more warriors.

Then she turned and marched back to her own VeinHolders. She was going to have to pull all the warriors that were out, waiting for Kinaki's warriors who'd slipped behind the border. They'd planned on capturing those warriors in a giant trap.

Now, she needed every sword at the front line.

And she might have to draw her own border back. What would happen if suddenly, they were a mile away?

Kinaki's troops would just chase after her, all the way back to the capital.

Maybe now that the House of Crystal had settled they would send aid.

Unnir knew it would still arrive too late.

Chapter Thirty-Six
HOUSE OF PEARL

CHUYOKO RELIED on every inch of her training to maintain a pleasant mien, to not bark orders or to tear the head off of anyone who had a question.

They could have won.

That phrase kept going through her head as she (gratefully) used magic to tear down tents, to gather up gear, to send messages to the far corners of the camp, getting everyone ready.

It was going to be a rough trip to the southern border of the lands of the House of Crystal. Though they were several days away from it, Darikuto was going to drain himself by throwing everyone else at the border in a single hour.

There would be no gentle walking. By the Goddess, the landing would probably be rough as well. Nothing would be organized. Chuyoko's equipment would be in good shape. She couldn't say that about the other warriors, those without the discipline to take care of their weapons each and every day.

She still wasn't going to say anything to them about it. Today wasn't the day.

Despite her efforts to stay pleasant, people got out of her way quickly when she walked up. Her anger was probably radiating off of her, like a black rock in the evening that had been baked all day in the sunlight.

They could have won.

Yes, it had been absurd trying to fight ghosts using steel and fists. The ghosts had laughed in their faces.

Then snuck a hand under their armor, finding cracks and crevices they could trickle into, solidly freezing the skin underneath. Or they'd fly up into the face of a warrior and scream, confusing the person, making them turn and hit at their closest neighbor instead of the real enemy.

But a few of the warriors had gotten the right idea, close to the end. They used their magic and limited landsense to grab hold of the ghosts. It wasn't easy—Chuyoko had never managed to do it—but a few had been able wrap their hands around the torso of a ghost and drain them, suck away all the magic that animated them.

Given enough time, Chuyoko and the others could have devised a system for fighting the ghosts.

But Darikuto had folded before then. He hadn't relied on his warriors when he should have. Instead, he made the decision to *talk* with Yimifut, the new LandHolder, when he could have held on, fought him off.

Followed The Plan and taken this land for himself.

The only consolation for Chuyoko was that Darikuto had promised to send all his warriors into battle with the true enemy, Kinaki. They weren't even going back to the lands of the House of Pearl.

She'd already sent messengers off, aided by Darikuto's magic to speed them along. They would raise the rest of the army and send it to the eastern border, then continue, into the lands of the House of Cobalt.

The boy, Yimifut, had warned that they were going to be too late. Unnir hadn't fallen, but probably would, soon.

Fighting a demon army that had just gotten their second wind, were rapidly stealing every bit of magic that they could from a newly possessed land…in some ways, Chuyoko wondered if these were the battles that she'd been preparing for her entire life.

While others might quake in their boots at the thought, Chuyoko found herself eager to go, to get there, to have a place to direct her anger.

It felt uncomfortable being so angry at Darikuto. He was her LandHolder. She'd followed him forever.

And yet… *They could have won.*

Chuyoko knew that Darikuto was already making changes to The Plan. She could tell by that look in his eyes that more, so much more was going on despite how busy he appeared to be, getting the camp ready to move.

Would he remember next time he faced a LandHolder to rely on his warriors?

Chuyoko doubted it.

And in return, had she just learned to stop relying on him?

Cast List

House of Crystal
  Nyati—Capitol
  Ibitsima—Former LandHolder
  Haptomi—Former head priest of the Temple of Truth
  Menhaptu—Current head priest of the Temple of Truth
  Akalina—Related to the LandHolder
  Befery—Akalina's sister
  Yimifut—Chosen of the Land
  CrsytalHolders—leaders of House of Crystal warriors
  Baka—Head of the CrystalHolders

House of Cobalt
  Jinyi—Capitol
  Kinaki—LandHolder
  Wanho—LandHolder's Demon
  Chaotu—LandHolder's son
  Lijun—LandHolder's daughter
  Belam—Former head priest of the Temple of Truth
  Sunli—Current head priest of the Temple of Truth
  CollierHolders—leaders of House of Cobalt warriors

House of Gold

Haravik—Capitol

Unnir—LandHolder

Torja—Head Priestess of the Temple of Truth

Ragna—Torja's assistant

Emil & Vide—Cousins of Unnir, children of Yudur, the former LandHolder

VeinHolders—leaders of House of Gold warriors

House of Pearl

Yawatan—Capitol

Kinaki—LandHolder

Shimokoro—Head of the Temple of Truth

Benitoyo—Merchant and spy

Chuyoko—Head of the warriors

Orinmegu—Chuyoko's second in command

PearlHolders—leaders of House of Pearl warriors

Read More!

Be sure to pick up all the books in the Houses of the Dead trilogy!

Houses Divided
Houses Fallen
Houses Reborn

Available at your favorite retailers!

About the Author

Leah Cutter writes page-turning fiction in exotic locations, such as a magical New Orleans, the ancient Orient, Hungary, the Oregon coast, rural Kentucky, Seattle, Minneapolis, and many others.

She writes literary, fantasy, mystery, science fiction, and horror fiction. Her short fiction has been published in magazines like *Alfred Hitchcock's Mystery Magazine* and *Talebones*, anthologies like Fiction River, and on the web. Her long fiction has been published both by New York publishers as well as small presses.

Find Leah's books on Knotted Road Press at (www.KnottedRoadPress.com)

Follow her blog at www.LeahCutter.com.

Reviews

It's true. Reviews help me sell more books. If you've enjoyed this story, please consider leaving a review of it on your favorite site.

Come someplace new...
Are you a traveler? Do you enjoy exploring strange new worlds, new cultures, new people?

Journey into the various lands envisioned by Leah Cutter.

Sign up for my newsletter and I'll start you on your travels with a free copy of my book, *The Island Sampler*.

I will never spam you or use your email for nefarious purposes. You can also unsubscribe at any time.

http://www.LeahCutter.com/newsletter/

About Knotted Road Press

Knotted Road Press fiction specializes in dynamic writing set in mysterious, exotic locations.

Knotted Road Press non-fiction publishes autobiographies, business books, cookbooks, and how-to books with unique voices.

Knotted Road Press creates DRM-free ebooks as well as high-quality print books for readers around the world.

With authors in a variety of genres including literary, poetry, mystery, fantasy, and science fiction, Knotted Road Press has something for everyone.

Knotted Road Press
www.KnottedRoadPress.com